MW01101469

YOUTHFUL INDISCRETIONS

YOUTHFUL INDISCRETIONS
ANONYMOUS

Carroll & Graf Publishers, Inc.
New York

Copyright © 1991 by Carroll & Graf Publishers, Inc.

First Carroll & Graf edition 1991

Carroll & Graf Publishers, Inc.
260 Fifth Avenue
New York, NY 10001

ISBN: 0-88184-778-X

Manufactured in the United States of America

YOUTHFUL INDISCRETIONS

Among all my school-fellows, there was no one to whom, especially after the departure of Hamilton, I felt so much attached as George Vivian. Several circumstances contributed to cement our intimacy, and we had not been long acquainted before we were on such a footing as to have no secrets from one another. I have already adverted to the favourable impression which his conduct towards me on the occasion of the flogging had produced upon my mind, and I was very desirous to do anything in my power to show him how much I had felt it.

He, too, was an orphan like myself, and having likewise been brought up almost entirely among ladies, he could enter into all my feelings better than most of our school-fellows, who had been accustomed to the amusements and sports of large families. In one respect he had at first an advantage of me, for though he had only been for a short time at the Doctor's he had previously been for a year at another school and, of course, was more up to the ways of school-boys than I was. He was clever and quick and had a most excellent memory, but unfortunately the school he had been at formerly was not well conducted and his teachers had been quite satisfied that he could repeat the lesson set him, without taking the trouble to ascertain whether he understood it or not. His natural cleverness enabled him to keep his place with most of his school-fellows at the Doctor's, but it was not long before I discovered my own superiority. I was quite convinced that if he chose to exert himself he could stand much higher in the school than he did. In most things where memory and quickness availed, he was not behind anyone, but what he failed in was where

3

it was necessary to apply to some purpose the rules which he had no difficulty in learning by heart, but of which it could hardly be said he knew the meaning. Above all things he felt his deficiency in the capacity of making verses, and he was constantly obliged to apply to some of his companions for assistance. After a short time, I was his principal resource, and though I would sometimes scold him for not trying to do them himself, I always cheerfully gave him all the assistance in my power.

One day, however, I asked him seriously whether he would not feel much happier if he could depend upon himself rather than be obliged to have recourse always to another for assistance. He was somewhat annoyed at first, and said that if I grudged the trouble he would not apply to me again.

I said it was not at all the trouble I thought of, as he knew quite well it was no trouble to me, but that I considered that with his abilities he might very easily learn to do them much better than I could, and that what I wanted to persuade him to do would, for a time at least, give me a great deal more trouble than making the verses myself.

He said it was no use to think of it, as he had often tried but never could succeed, though he admitted that he felt greatly annoyed at his inferiority in this respect to others who were greatly below him in most subjects.

I at length persuaded him to allow me to attempt to explain to him the rules, which he could repeat but the meaning and application of which he had never thoroughly understood, and he agreed to devote a certain time every day to this purpose. It was at first rather a hard struggle as it obliged us for a time to abandon some of our amusements, and he was several times on the point of giving up the attempt. In the course of a few weeks, however, he began to have a glimpse of what I wanted to impress upon him, and thenceforward he was as anxious as I could be to prosecute our private studies. It seemed to come upon him like a flash of lightning, and he could not imagine, when he first began to see the light, how it was that he had remained so long in

4

the dark.

The change in him was so great that it attracted the attention of the Doctor, who had not previously done justice to his abilities; his commendations not only gratified George, but encouraged him to exert himself still more.

His gratitude to me for having thus drawn forth his powers and made him conscious of his own abilities was extreme, and there was nothing he would not have done to convince me how strong this feeling was.

We used often to talk about our previous histories and compare our thoughts and feelings. He had lost his parents at an early age, and had been brought up by his grandmother – a stern, though not unkind old lady. She resided in a curious old mansion which had formerly been an Abbey, and the only inmates of the family were a maiden daughter, approaching fifty years of age, and two young ladies, one a year and the other a few months younger than George.

These young ladies were not related to him, being relatives of his grandmother's second husband. They were both well provided for, but being without any near relations they had lived under the charge of his grandmother as long as he could recollect.

Of these girls he would never tire of speaking, and he soon gave me the details of everything that had passed with them. He had no companions of his own sex, and his whole time was spent with them. They shared the lessons in Greek and Latin which he received from the curate of the parish, and he, in turn, participated in their French, Italian, music and dancing lessons, for which masters attended from a neighbouring town.

Their schoolroom was a large apartment, somewhat detached from the house, which had formerly been the chapel of the Abbey. As from its situation any noise they made there did not disturb the inhabitants of the rest of the house, this apartment gradually came to be their usual resort and the scene of all their indoor amusements. The greater part of the walls were covered with book presses, which were kept locked and from which they occasionally persuaded their aunt to allow them to take a few books, such as she approved of. As they grew older, however, and became fond of reading, they longed to become better acquainted with the contents of the bookshelves.

Luckily George discovered a key which opened the presses and enabled them to gratify their curiosity. For some time they indulged themselves, to their great delight, with the perusal of *Tom Jones, Peregrine Pickle*, and some other works of the old school which had been carefully concealed from them, but with which they were highly diverted.

One day they made a discovery which, at first, startled them not a little. While replacing some books on an upper shelf, George allowed one to get behind the others, and leaning forward to pick it up, his foot slipped, and he nearly fell from the chair. This made him press forcibly against the bookshelf, and in doing so he touched a secret spring, upon which the shelf started forward and disclosed a small recess behind.

Their curiosity was of course excited to ascertain what the hiding place contained, and they discovered two or three old books, which, from the dust on them, had evidently not been touched for many years. They turned out on inspection to be some collections of erotic plates from the Académie des Dames, Aretino, and other works of a similar description.

Their astonishment on seeing these may be imagined; George was delighted with them, and attracted by the sight of the naked figures and the strange attitudes, he wished to examine them minutely; but the girls said they were not proper to be looked at, and insisted on putting them back. George, however, was not satisfied with this hasty glance, but used often to return to them by himself and pore over them, wondering what their meaning could be.

Before long, too, he became aware, from noticing that the position of the books was sometimes changed that, though the girls had professed to him their dislike to look at them,

6

they also were in the habit of amusing themselves with them in secret. To make certain of this, he one day concealed himself beneath the sofa, and when he found them employed in examining the plates, he made his appearance and, somewhat to their confusion, rallied them upon their pretended modesty, which he now found was no greater safeguard against their curiosity than his own.

After this there could be no further disguise on the subject amongst them, and they used often to take the books down, examine the pictures, and discuss their different ideas and conjectures as to the purposes and meanings of the various attitudes. This led before long to a comparison between the beauties of the figures thus represented, and those of the similar parts which they themselves possessed. George vowed that he was certain the girls were much handsomer than any of the personages represented on the plates, and insisted on satisfying himself on the point, but they at first resisted his attempts to gratify this very natural curiosity.

One day, when they were discussing the strange appearance of the virile member as represented in a state of erection, George took courage and, letting down his trousers, exhibited to them his little bijou, with all its surrounding attributes, that they might compare it with the representation.

They pretended at first to be shocked, but curiosity and desire soon got the better of every other feeling, so that, after he had induced them to explore all his secret charms, he had not much difficulty in persuading them to gratify him by exposing in turn all the beauties they had to show.

The ice having been once broken, this soon became their constant amusement when they had a safe opportunity for indulging in it. But at this time they were all too young to be able to comprehend, and still less to put in practice, the lessons which were thus exhibited to them.

In imitation of the scenes depicted in the plates, George would get between their thighs and endeavour to introduce his little member, which their caresses had made quite stiff, within their secret recesses; but as the attempt to insert it always occasioned pain to them, and was not accompanied by any corresponding increase of pleasure to George, they soon gave up attempting what appeared to them to be something preposterous, and contented themselves with toying with and kissing and caressing each other's secret charms.

At first the total absence of hair from the parts of their own bodies, which they saw depicted in the engravings as surrounded with curly locks, occasioned them some amazement; but in the course of time it became evident that Eliza, the elder of the cousins, was beginning to give proof positive that this was not an exaggeration of the artist, as they had at first supposed. Her bubbies too began to swell out, and her mount to increase in size, and George found that when he tickled and played with her little secret part, she now exhibited more evident tokens of pleasure and enjoyment.

His own pretty jewel too was now becoming more and more excited, and was increasing considerably in size, while the two little appendages began to show themselves more prominently depending from the belly, and hanging down as he saw them represented in the pictures.

In short, matters were fast progressing in the natural train, so as to bring on with them the age of puberty, and a very short time longer would no doubt have sufficed not only to render them capable, but to supply the desires which would induce them to carry out experiments far enough to initiate them into the whole secret; but to their infinite sorrow and regret, their pleasant party was suddenly dispersed.

George's grandmother, Mrs Montague, had another daughter who had been for some time residing abroad. She had recently been attacked with a dangerous illness, which threatened to be of long continuance; and at her urgent request, Mrs Montague had been induced to break up her establishment at the Abbey, and proceed with her unmarried daughter to join the invalid in Italy.

This, of course, involved a complete separation between George and his fair companions. After a sorrowful parting, the girls went to a boarding school, and George was also sent to a school, where he was so uncomfortable that at length he petitioned to be removed. To his great joy this was agreed to; and he went to the Doctor's, where he had only been for a few months when I joined him.

When we became intimate, nothing rejoiced him so much as to talk of the girls, and many a long conversation we had regarding them, when he would detail to me all the minute particulars of what had passed between them, and bitterly regret his own ignorance and want of ability to avail himself of the pleasure which he now thought he might have enjoyed; and he looked forward with the greatest eagerness to the enjoyment he anticipated when he should again have the happiness of meeting them.

It was some years before he was to have that joy. One day towards the end of our schooldays together, he gleefully handed me an open letter. It was from his grandmother, who a short time previously had returned to the Abbey, and contained an invitation for him to spend the summer holidays with her. She mentioned that he would meet his old friends Eliza and Maria, who had again come to reside with her, and told him that if he wished he might bring one of his school-fellows with him as a companion. His object was now to induce me to accompany him on this visit, and to participate with him in all the enjoyments he anticipated on meeting his two old friends.

Although I was by no means quite so sanguine as he was of our being at once admitted to all his previous intimacy, still I was very anxious to see the girls of whom I had heard so much, and readily agreed to his proposal, thinking that what had previously happened gave us a fair reason to hope that even all his anticipations might be realised.

Accordingly, on the appointed day, having made ourselves as smart as possible, we arrived at the Abbey. It was near the dinner hour when we reached it, and we were received by his grandmother – a stately though by no means

9

disagreeable dame – who told us that we had just time to get ready for dinner.

We proceeded to decorate ourselves as quickly as possible; and like young fools, as we then were, we fancied that we would be most likely to make an impression by affecting as much as possible the appearance and manners of the man. When we met the family party in the drawing room, I was greatly struck with the beauty of the two girls, and could not help acknowledging that the glowing description George had so often given of them was by no means an exaggeration of the reality.

The impression made upon me by our reception was of the most favourable description; but with poor George it was quite the reverse. Being an utter stranger I could expect nothing beyond civility, and I was not at all surprised at the coldness with which the girls received me. George, whose impressions of their former intimacy were just as vivid as if they had only separated the day previously, had calculated upon being received exactly on the same footing as that on which they had parted. And on going up to them with open arms, he was horrified to find that he was received upon the same cold and frigid terms which were accorded to me.

He was sadly mortified at this cool treatment and at finding that all his advances were met with the utmost reserve, while he was addressed as Mr. George and I as Sir Francis, on every occasion.

Poor George could not conceal his mortification, and with difficulty prevented the tears from gushing from his eyes at the sad contrast which this reception presented to the delightful interview he had pictured to himself. I, of course, had never anticipated anything else so far as I was concerned but I was more at my ease, and consequently able to observe matters more calmly. It struck me that there was something forced and overdone in the manner in which the girls were acting; and that it looked rather as if they were afraid of themselves and were obliged to resort to all this formality to prevent their showing their real feelings.

While, therefore, I was polite and attentive to them, I

devoted myself almost exclusively to the old ladies, upon whom I was desirous to produce a good impression, directing my conversations chiefly to them and avoiding in this manner any appearance of being too anxious to make myself agreeable to the young ladies.

In this way I was enabled to make my observations on their demeanour more easily and without attracting attention. As the evening wore on, matters did not improve so far as George was concerned. The same cold and formal stiffness was still kept up towards him. Once, when we were left alone with the young ladies he summoned up courage, and on some pretext took an opportunity of passing his arm round Maria's waist, but he was instantly met with a sharp 'Come, come, behave yourself, sir; we must not have any of your school-boy tricks here.'

Poor George was quite abashed at such an unexpected rejoinder, and hardly ventured to open his mouth again during the evening. I, however, rattled away as well as I could, and did my best to amuse the old ladies, and made things pass off pleasantly.

At George's suggestion we had been accommodated in two adjoining apartments, which he had formerly occupied, and which were situated in a semidetached wing abutting on the library.

When we had retired to our rooms for the night, George was quite frantic at the manner in which he had been treated, and was half inclined to be angry with me for taking the matter so coolly as I did; and now, when he could freely give way to his feelings, the tears which he had hitherto had some difficulty in suppressing rolled down his cheeks. I had been disposed to rally him a little on his disappointment, but when I saw how seriously he took it to heart, I had not the cruelty to add to his annoyance, and proceeded to try to console him a little. I reminded him that now more than five years had elapsed since he and his fair friends had met.

During that period he had acquired a good deal of experience and knowledge of the world, and it was only reasonable to suppose that the girls also must have made similar progress. That during all this time they had had no opportunity of ascertaining what his views and feelings were, beyond the exchange of a few formal letters which were necessarily very guarded on both sides; and that it was hardly reasonable to expect that they should at once throw themselves into his arms – a proceeding which they might naturally suppose would appear to him more like the conduct of two prostitutes than anything else, and more likely to disgust him than otherwise.

He admitted that there was some truth in this, and that he had expected too much at first. But he was much more relieved when I proceeded to tell him the opinion I had formed, that in their conduct this evening the girls were only acting a part. I related to him some observations I had made, which led me to think that my first supposition to this effect was correct.

What chiefly satisfied him was one circumstance I had remarked while I was playing chess with Miss Vivian, and they thought I was not observing them. George was standing opposite us, looking over a portfolio of engravings which his grandmother had brought from the Continent. While turning them over he raised his foot upon a chair to support the portfolio, the light was shining strong upon his figure, and the proportions of his manly appendage were plainly exhibited.

Poor George was thinking less of the engravings he was turning over, than of those he had been accustomed in former days to amuse himself with, along with his fair companions, and this caused the unruly member to be in rather an excited state. Its full development attracted the attention of Maria, who, with a smile, pointed it out to Eliza, and a meaningful look passed between them as if they were well pleased to see such a change upon it.

All this byplay did not escape by observation, though they thought I was too intent on my game to observe it, and from George's position he could not be at all conscious that he was the object of their attention.

What I thus told George comforted him very much, and

with some anxiety he asked my advice as to what we ought to do in the circumstances in which we found ourselves, so different from what he had expected. I told him I was afraid we had made a mistake in trying, as we had done, to play the young gentlemen, and that we had thereby given them too good an opportunity of keeping us at a distance, which they would hardly have been able to do if we had come down upon them in the character of two riotous school-boys. I said that it was perhaps not yet too late to rectify the error, and that as Miss Maria had chosen to refer to school-boy tricks, it was worth while to try, at least, whether we could not play some upon them to good effect. He said he was willing to do anything I thought best, as nothing could be more unsatisfactory than our present position. We therefore determined on our course, and after consoling one another in the best way we could for our present disappointment, we fell asleep.

The next morning, discarding broadcloth and silks, jewellery and French polish, we made our appearance at breakfast in short jackets, trousers of plain woolen stuff, fitting close to our waist and haunches, open breasted waist coats, and our necks merely encircled with a light handkerchief loosely tied in front. I cannot so well say what this effect had upon myself, though I had no reason to suppose from George's compliments on my appearance that it was unfavourable. But in so far as he was concerned, I could not help thinking that it was a great improvement, and that he now looked to be much more likely to captivate a girl's fancy than he had appeared to be on the previous evening, when dressed up to the highest pitch of the then youthful fashion. Like myself he had rather a young appearance for his age. This suited our purpose well, and I had little doubt we should be able to pass ourselves off in the character we had assumed.

Perhaps a close observer would have remarked that our forms were more rounded, and our muscles more prominent than was reconcilable with our assumed youthful appearance; but this was not likely to be much noticed in

13

the quarter where alone we cared about making a good impression. Our only fear was that our thin, tight-fitting trousers might betray to the elder ladies the secret of our manly organs having arrived at a size and proportion likely to render us dangerous companions for two young girls.

But we resolved to be cautious in our movements and proceedings before them, for there had been an object in our purposely selecting these garments – in order that without appearing to make any display, we might have an opportunity of exhibiting to the young ladies, as if accidentally, on every possible occasion that there was something beneath them which was likely to prove an agreeable and satisfactory plaything, if they would only throw off their reserve and give us an excuse for producing them for their amusement.

During breakfast, George and I talked of nothing but the sporting amusements which we looked forward to enjoying in the country; and as soon as the meal was over he insisted on carrying me off to the river to fish, where we remained all day till dinner time.

I thought I observed some slight indications of disappointment at our course of procedure; but as this was exactly what we wished, we were encouraged to pursue our plan.

During the evening I devoted myself as before, almost exclusively to the old ladies; and George, who had somewhat recovered his spirits, amused himself with occasionally teasing the younger ones a little, at the same time taking every opportunity he could find of allowing them, as if accidentally, to catch a glimpse of the proportions of a certain weapon, which he eagerly longed to make use of, and which every now and them he made to erect itself and, as if unconsciously on his part, to appear prominently beneath his trousers.

On more than one occasion, when he contrived to do this in such a position that they thought he could not observe them, I noticed the same meaningful look of satisfaction pass between the girls which I had observed the previous

14

evening. Upon the whole, we were convinced that everything was now proceeding as satisfactorily as we could expect.

The next morning at breakfast we continued the same game, and George again proposed some expedition which would occupy the whole day; but here his grandmother interfered and said, 'Come, come, George, this will never do. You must not engross Sir Francis so entirely, you see enough of him at school, and you must allow us to have a little of his company while he is here. Why, here are the two young ladies who have been putting off any distant excursion all the summer, until they should have somebody to escort them about.'

George and I exchanged a quiet look of satisfaction at this exposé, and at once said that if the ladies would accept of our services, we were quite at their command whenever they chose.

They, on their part, disclaimed any wish to interfere with our amusements, but Mrs Montague again struck in and said, 'Well, George, you and Sir Francis can occupy yourselves in any way you like till lunch time. After that I shall order the horses to be at the door, and you can take him to see the old castle. If you have forgot the way, the ladies will be able to show it to you.'

After lunch, we accordingly set off on an expedition to some ruins about ten miles off. As it was by no means our plan to remain on a distant footing with our friends, when we had them by ourselves we both endeavoured by all means in our power, when thus thrown into close contact with them, to make ourselves as agreeable as possible.

Before long we separated into two pairs, George taking Maria who was just of his own age, and leaving Eliza for me. I believe we both at first took the same mode of proceeding – that of praising each other, being pretty well assured that what we said of one another would not fail to be repeated by the listener to her friend.

I soon found myself rapidly improving my intimacy with Eliza, who was not only an extremely handsome, but an accomplished girl; and I strove, not without some success, to make myself as agreeable as possible to her, though of course I at first preserved the utmost respect in my manner, so as not to alarm her.

When we reached the ruins we put up our horses and walked about, in order to inspect them, thoroughly. George and Maria soon separated from us. Eliza sat down to take a sketch of the ruins, and after sitting talking to her for a while, I also drew out my sketchbook, and took up my position a little behind her, imitating her example.

While thus occupied, I could occasionally hear from the merry tones they made use of that George and Maria were getting on at a most satisfactory rate. At length, when I had nearly completed my sketch, and was filling in the foreground with the outline of Eliza's figure, they came up behind us, and looking over my shoulder, Maria exclaimed, 'Oh, Sir Francis, how beautiful that is! I should so like to have it, it is such a capital likeness of Eliza. Oh, pray, do give it to me.'

I answered, 'By all means! But upon one condition, and that is that you will persuade Miss Eliza to give me in exchange her sketch, as a remembrance of the place.'

Having heard what passed, Eliza now turned round to us, and on looking at my drawing, she said that Maria might do anything she liked with hers as it was not good for anything, and she would make a much better one by copying mine. The exchange was accordingly made.

Seeing that there were some other sketches in my book, they asked to be allowed to look at them. I appeared to hesitate and said that I was not quite sure I could permit this, that they must recollect a school-boy's sketchbook was generally filled with everything that came in his way which struck his fancy, sometimes without much regard to propriety.

In fact, the very reason why I had selected this book was that among other things, it contained several sketches of George and myself, taken when we were bathing, and exhibiting our naked figures at full length. There was nothing absolutely indecent in them, either in the attitudes or even in the form and position of the Priapean member, but there was no attempt to conceal it, and it was exhibited in its full natural proportions when in a state of rest, with its shading of foliage, as yet but scanty, around it. My hesitation only excited their curiosity the more; and though Eliza said little, Maria pressed me to show them anything I thought I could.

I then turned over the leaves, allowing them to look at some of the other sketches, and when I came to those of ourselves, I at first folded down part of the leaf and only exhibited the upper portion of our persons naked as far as the navel.

Though they made no observation, I saw from their flushed cheeks how much they were affected by the sight; and when they came to one or two sketches where our virile members were not so prominently displayed, although sufficiently indicated, I allowed them to see them, affecting to do so through awkwardness in turning over the leaves. When they had gone over the whole they expressed their admiration and their thanks; and we soon after mounted our horses to return home.

While getting the horses out, George found an opportunity to tell me what I had already guessed from the expression on his face, that he had got on even better than he had expected with Maria. That though she would not allow him to take any serious liberty, he thought this arose more from the fear of being observed than from unwillingness on her part; and he had even been able more than once to place his hand upon his old darling friend, now clothed in a new dress; and had made her grasp and feel the increased proportions of his throbbing weapon.

This was as much as we could possibly expect and emboldened by what he told me, I ventured while raising Eliza into the saddle and adjusting her dress, to press her leg and bottom, and even to insinuate my hand under the riding habit and touch the naked, soft, smooth skin of her thigh, without meeting with either rebuke or resistance.

We had a merry ride home, and during dinner all were in high spirits. George, especially, was so much so that it attracted the observation of his grandmother, who made some remark upon it; to which he replied that he had formerly been so scolded for being a madcap, that he had been trying for the last two days to see if he could not gain a better character, but that he found it was of no use to make the attempt, and he must just submit to the reproach.

This produced a smile, and the evening passed on very pleasantly. For the first time since our arrival, the piano was opened, and the young ladies gave us some music. They both had good voices, and sang well; but they wanted that taste and polish which can only be acquired by hearing first-rate performers. I had had great advantages in that way in consequence of my mother's fondness for music, which was almost the only amusement she ever indulged in. During our visits to London, she was not only a regular attendant at the Opera, but was in the constant habit of having at her house all the highest talent of musical celebrity. George, too, had one of the finest voices I have ever heard, and latterly, at least, he had had the advantage of a most excellent master.

I was engaged with Miss Vivian in a game of chess, when I heard Maria say to George, 'Well, George, I suppose you have entirely forgotten all the lessons in music I used to take so much pains to give you.'

George laughed, but I answered for him, 'No, indeed, Miss Maria, I can assure you he has not at all forgotten them, and I am quite sure you will find you have no reason to be ashamed of your pupil.'

She insisted that from the way in which I spoke, I must be musical myself, and that she must get me to sing to her, as she was sure I was a much better performer than George. I replied that I would not at all deny that I was fond of music, and would be glad to do anything I could to contribute to their amusement, more especially as I saw it was useless to struggle any longer with Miss Vivian, who was just about to checkmate me, but that I must make one

18

condition, which was that I was to be allowed to make my exhibition first, as I was quite sure that after they had heard George they would never have patience to listen to me.

I had by this time learned that it was sometimes politic to allow one's self to be occasionally beaten, even at chess, and I very soon allowed Miss Vivian to win the game, and then joined the musical party.

I selected a song that had Eliza's name upon it. Maria smiled, and called to Eliza that it was one of her songs and she must come and play it, which she accordingly did. I tried to do my best, and certainly had no reason to be dissatisfied with the commendations which I received and, at their request, I gave them two or three more, which they suggested. I then resigned my place to George.

Maria offered to play for him, but he said he would rather accompany himself, and took his seat at the piano. He played the prelude to the beautiful air 'Una furtiva Lagrima,' and then commenced to sing. For the first few notes his voice rather wavered, but he soon regained his confidence, and poured out a strain of exquisite music in the most charming manner. Even I, who had been in the constant habit of hearing him sing, was surprised at the manner in which he acquitted himself, but animated by the presence of those he loved, he was evidently induced to exert himself to the utmost, and certainly he did succeed in creating a most powerful sensation. Long before he had finished, there was not a dry eye in the room. Even Mrs Montague, usually so impassive, was roused from her imposing gravity. She first laid down her book to listen, and then rose from her seat and came and stood behind George.

When he had finished, there was perfect silence for a minute or two, and then his grandmother, who was the first to recover herself, said, 'George, my dear boy, I knew you had a fine voice, but I had no idea it would have improved so greatly. You must have practised a great deal to have become so perfect. I hope it has not been at the expense of your other studies.'

I here struck in, 'No, indeed, Mrs Montague. I can assure

19

you that it has not, and I am certain if you apply to the Doctor, he will tell you the same thing. I know some people think a taste for music is a dangerous one and likely to lead one into bad society, and it may be so with some, but I am quite sure it has had quite a different effect with us; it has often amused us, and kept us out of company where we might not have been so well employed.'

'I am very glad to hear it,' she replied, 'and I hope this will always be the case. But where did you contrive to improve yourself so much, George? I was not aware you had taken lessons in music.'

'Why,' answered George, 'my two first instructors, to whom I owe most, are both present.'

'Indeed,' said I, 'you owe everything to Miss Maria. At one time, I certainly had the presumption to fancy I could give you some instruction, but I soon found that the pupil was far before the master, though I suspect that neither of us would have made much progress latterly, had it not been for the kindness of the worthy signor.'

'And pray who is the signor?' asked Maria.

'Why, he is an Italian nobleman – a refugee, whose acquaintance I made some time ago. His story is too long to detail here, though I shall give it you some day for it is a very curious one; but he considered he was under some obligation to me for getting my uncle to use his interest with some influential people in his favour, so as to save the remnant of his property, and he took a great fancy to George, which has induced him to devote a good deal of time and trouble to our instruction.'

George was then requested to give them another song, which he did at once, and we continued the musical entertainment during the evening, taking care to make the young ladies join with us, so as to avoid any appearance of wishing to show off.

At the end of one of George's songs, I heard Maria say in a low tone, 'Oh, George! George! How could you be here for two whole days without giving us this pleasure?'

'It is all your own fault,' retorted he. 'You snubbed me so

much the first night I came, that I have been afraid ever since even to open my mouth.'

When we retired to bed in the evening we congratulated ourselves on the success of our plan, feeling satisfied that we had made as much progress as we could have expected under the circumstances. In the morning, too, we had another proof of the effect we had produced on the girls. On returning from our ride the previous afternoon, I had pretended to hide my sketchbook in the pocket of my overcoat, which was hanging up in the hall, taking care that Maria should see where I put it. On looking at it in the morning, we found that it was not only quite apparent that it had been inspected, but that two of the sketches – those which gave the most complete and perfect representations of our organs of manhood – were wanting, and had evidently been cut out by our young friends. As a good many other pages had been taken out in the same manner, they probably though the theft would never have been discovered, but I knew quite well what was there, and could not be mistaken on the subject.

We of course took no notice of this, but we thought it was a complete demonstration of their inclinations, and we determined that we should now take the first opportunity in our power to bring them to such terms as would enable us to procure the pleasure we desired to share with them.

The day turned out to be very wet, and we made an excuse of this to remain in the house and cultivate our intimacy with the girls. After breakfast, Maria said, 'Well, George, will you come to the drawing room, and pay me back some of the music lessons I used to give you?'

'With all my heart,' said George, 'There is nothing would give me greater pleasure that to practice *all* the lessons you used to teach me.'

She blushed and seemed a little confused, but immediately led the way to the drawing room, where we spent a couple of hours practising over all the old songs they had been accustomed to sing together. At last I said, 'Why, George, this will never do. If we continue at this rate we shall exhaust all our stores, and shall never be able to create a sensation again.'

George, however, did not seem disposed to leave the piano, apparently thinking that his position, bending over Maria, gave him a favourable opportunity for a little fingering upon a still more delicate instrument than the one she was performing upon.

I wished to leave the field there clear for him and therefore turned to Eliza, who was sitting with her back turned to them, netting a purse.

'Oh, this is exactly what I wanted,' said I. 'I want to make a landing net, but I am afraid I have quite forgotten how to form the meshes. Perhaps you will be good enough to give me a lesson.'

She at once assented. I brought my materials and sat down beside her. She soon discovered that I knew quite as much on the subject as she did, but she said nothing, and continued to give me all the instruction I applied for, apparently not objecting to the use I made of the opportunity afforded me of pressing her hand and taking a few other liberties with her person.

In the meantime I kept up the conversation, which soon turned upon the subject of the Abbey. I said I felt myself quite at home there and could hardly persuade myself that I had entered it for the first time only three days before; I told her that George had been so fond of talking of it, and of describing everything that had occurred to him in it, that I believed I was almost as well acquainted with it as himself, for I was quite sure there was not a room in the house he had been in, not a book he had read, not a picture he had looked at, which he had not described over and over again.

As I said this in rather a marked tone, I saw Eliza's cheeks become suffused with a deep blush, and heard Maria whisper to George, 'Oh, George! George! How could you?'

'Never do you mind,' was his reply. 'He is quite safe: you need not be afraid of him.'

I took no notice of this, and soon changed the subject, adverting to our school days, and to all we had done for one

22

another. Among other things I told them the only time we had ever got into a regular scrape was because we had refused to tell upon each other, and preferred to submit to a flogging rather than bring each other into disgrace.

At the mention of flogging they seemed greatly interested, and Maria especially pricked up her ears and put some questions on the subject as to how often we had been subjected to it and how we liked it. Seeing that they were amused with what I told them, I continued, greatly to George's diversion, to entertain them with sundry accounts of floggings, some of which were purely imaginary and the others improvements upon scenes that had actually occurred, not with ourselves, but with some of our acquaintances.

I gradually wound up their curiosity to a high pitch and Maria especially seemed to take a great interest in the subject. Observing this, I went on to say that it was a matter which one could convey no adequate idea of by mere description, and that to understand it properly it was necessary to have gone through it, or at least to have witnessed the operation itself. 'I only wish,' said I, 'that I had you at school some day when it was going on, that you might see the thing regularly carried through.'

Maria here burst out with 'Oh! it would be so funny to see it.'

'Well,' said I, 'I am afraid there is no possibility of conveying you to school for that purpose, but here is George, who is such a perfect ladies' man, that I am quite sure if he thought it would afford you any amusement he would at once submit to undergo the operation, in order merely to give you an idea of how it is done, and for my part, I shall be quite willing to act the part of the school-master, and apply the birch in a satisfactory manner.'

'Speak for yourself,' said George, 'I am not a bit fonder of it than you are.'

The girls burst out in a fit of laughter, and I gave George a look which he at once understood as a hint to keep up the

23

joke. I continued to banter him, alleging that he was afraid of the pain and that he had not courage enough to stand the punishment.

Maria chimed in, and encouraged me to go on. After some little jesting on the subject, George appeared to come round, and at length agreed that he would submit to go through the ceremony of being flogged in their presence, exactly as the operation would be performed at school. He said the only think he did not like about the punishment was the being kept in suspense, and he therefore stipulated that there should be no delay, and that the affair should be brought to a conclusion at once. I said there was but one objection to this, which was that as the punishment was to be bona fide and not in joke, there was a risk that he might make an outcry which would disturb the house and get us into a scrape.

He affected to take this in high dudgeon, and to be greatly offended at the idea that he would cry out for such a trifle, and made an excuse of it for insisting that the affair should go on, in order to prove that he did not care in the least for the pain. At length he said that if we had any apprehension on this account it might easily be obviated by our going to the old schoolroom, where any noise that might be made could not be heard in the rest of the house.

At this allusion to the schoolroom, the girls exchanged a glance of alarm, and I hastened to remove any suspicion by saying it would be better to delay until the weather improved, when the scene could take place in the open air, at a distance from the house. George, however, insisted that there should be no delay, and at length a compromise was made by which it was arranged that if the rain ceased after luncheon we should go into the park, and if not, the ceremony should take place in the schoolroom.

As the day wore on without any symptom of improvement, George and I made all the necessary preparations. After lunch, we sat for some time with the girls without referring to the subject, which occupied all our thoughts. At length Maria made an allusion to it, upon which George

24

started up and insisted on its being got over at once.

The so-called schoolroom – or rather library – was a large oblong apartment, which had formerly been the chapel of the Abbey. At one end was the principal entrance, and at the other a large bay window, which occupied the whole of that end of the room, with the exception of a closet on each side. The portion within the recess was elevated by two steps from the rest of the floor, and the window, though on the ground floor, was thus so high that no one on the outside could look into the room without getting up on the window sill, which, though not impossible, as George and I had already ascertained, was not an easy matter without some assistance. In the centre of the room was a long library table. A great portion of one side was taken up with a large fireplace; the remainder, and the whole of the opposite side, was occupied by bookshelves, while beside the table and opposite the fireplace, was a large old-fashioned sofa, more like a bed than a sofa of modern times.

When we reached the room I at once took upon myself the character of schoolmaster, and George assumed that of the pert school-boy. I placed the girls on the sofa, and drew a large stand for holding maps across the space between the sofa and the table, thus cutting off the communication between them and the door.

I then told George to prepare for punishment. He inquired, in a flippant tone, if he was to strip entirely naked. I pretended to be shocked, and answered with a serious air, 'No, sir; you know quite well that if I were about to punish you in a severe manner I should not expose you before your companions; but take care, sir, and do not provoke me too far; for though kissing a pretty girl is a grave fault and deserves the punishment you are about to undergo, still, disrespect to your master is a much greater crime, and if you continue to show it in this manner, I shall be obliged, however unwillingly, to resort to the severest punishment in my power to inflict.'

I then made him take off his coat and waistcoat, and pretended to fasten my hands above his head to the roller from which the maps depended. I then turned his handsome bottom to the girls, and taking up a birch rod which I had provided, I affected to flog his posteriors severely. He writhed and twisted his body in the most ridiculous manner, as if he was suffering greatly from the infliction of the blows, but at the same time he turned round his head, made wry faces, put out his tongue, and made fun to the girls, who were in fits of laughter and heartily enjoying the whole scene.

I rebuked him for his improper conduct, and told him that if it was continued, I must resort to severer measures with him. The more I appeared to get angry, the more he made game of me and the more outrageous he became. At length I approached him, and took hold of one hand, as if for the purpose of restraining his antics, and making him keep still, in order that I might be better able to apply the rod; but my object was of a totally different nature. I had taken care that he should have no braces on, and his trousers were merely fastened in front by two or three buttons. These I secretly unloosened, and having satisfied myself that his beautiful organ of manhood was in a sufficiently imposing state for the exhibition I meditated, I suddenly slipped down his trousers, raised up his shirt and inflicted two or three sharp blows on his naked posteriors, pure and white as snow, saying. 'There sir, since you will have it in this manner, how do you like it so?'

I had no sooner finished than he turned round, and as I took good care to hold his shirt well up, he exhibited to the astonished eyes of the two girls an object which they have often contemplated before, but certainly never in such a beautiful or satisfactory state. There it stood bolt upright, issuing from the tender curls which had begun to adorn it, with the curious little balls, as yet unshaded with hair, but of a slightly darker colour than the rest of his person, which made them show off in contrast with the pure white of his thighs, the pillar rearing itself proudly up towards his navel, surmounted with its lovely coral head.

The whole proceeding only occupied a few seconds, and

took the girls entirely by surprise. Uttering a shriek, they started up, and endeavoured to reach the door. This movement, however, had been foreseen, and as in order to arrive at it they had to go round the table, George was enabled to reach it before them. He hastily locked it, took out the key, and then planted himself before it, with his shirt tucked up round his waist, and his trousers down to his knees, exhibiting his flaming priapus as a formidable bar to their exit, while he exclaimed, 'No, no! You shan't escape in this manner. You have all had your share in the amusement, and it is now my turn to have mine, and not one of you shall leave the room till you have all undergone the same punishment as I have been subjected to. Come, Frank, this is all your doing, so I must begin with you.'

'By all means,' replied I, 'it shall never be said that I proposed to any one else what I was afraid to undergo myself.'

Prepared as I was for the scene, not a moment was lost. In a trice, my jacket and waistcoat were off, my trousers were down at my heels, and my shirt tucked up round my waist like George's, presenting, I flattered myself, as favourable a proof of my manly prowess as he had done. Taking up the rod, he applied a few stripes to my naked posteriors, while we watched the proceedings of the girls.

Finding their escape by the principal door barred by the flaming falchion which George brandished in their faces, they made an attempt to escape by the side door. This also had been guarded against. Ascertaining that it was locked, and now catching a glimpse of the new formidable weapon, which I disclosed to their sight, and which George took care should be presented in full view, they retreated to the sofa, covered their faces with their hands, and kneeling down, ensconced themselves in each corner, burying their heads in the cushions.

In this position, though they secured the main approach to the principal scene of pleasure which they probably supposed would be the first object of attack, they forgot that the back entrance was left quite open to assault. Nor were we

27

now all disposed to give them quarter. While George threw himself upon Maria, I made an attack upon Eliza.

Before they were aware what we are about their petticoats were turned up and their lovely bottoms exposed to our delighted gaze. Although we did not profane with the rod, a few slaps with our hands upon the polished ivory surfaces made them glow with a beauteous rosy tint. Ashamed of this exposure, they struggled to replace their petticoats. Nor was I at all unwilling to change the mode of attack. Throwing one arm round Eliza's waist to keep her down, and pressing my lips between her cheek, I inserted my hand beneath her petticoats as she attempted to pull them down, and gliding it up between her legs, I brought it by one rapid and decisive sweep fairly between her thighs to the very entrance, and even insinuated one finger within the lips, of the centre of attraction, before she was in the least aware of the change in my tactics.

She struggled at first, and endeavoured to rise up and get away from me. But I had secured my advantage too well to be easily defeated, and after a few unavailing attempts she gave up the contest, and seemed to resign herself to her fate.

I was not slow to avail myself of the advantage I had thus gained and, after kissing away a few tears, I contrived to insert the hand, with which I did not now find it necessary to hold her down, within the front of her gown, and proceeded to handle and toy with a most lovely pair of little, smooth, firm, bubbies, which seemed to grow harder under my burning touches.

All this time I continued to move my finger up and down in the most lascivious manner within the narrow entrance of the charming grotto into which I had managed to insert it, and the double action soon began to produce an evident effect upon her. The tears ceased to flow, and my ardent kisses, if not returned, were at least received with tokens of approbation and pleasure. Presently I felt the lips of her delicious recess contract and close upon my lascivious finger, and after a little apparent hesitation the buttocks began to move gently backwards and forwards in unison with the stimulating motions of the provoking intruder. Encouraged by this and feeling convinced that her voluptuous sensations were now carrying her ownward in the path of pleasure in spite of herself, I took hold of her hand and placed it upon my burning weapon. At first she attempted to withdraw it, but I held it firmly upon the throbbing and palpitating object; and after a little struggle I prevailed upon her not only to grasp it, but also to humour the wanton movements which I made with it backwards and forwards within the grasp of her soft fingers. This delightful amusement occupied us for some little time, and I was in no hurry to bring it to a close, for I found Eliza was every moment getting more and more excited, and her actions becoming freer and less embarrassed. But I felt that if I continued it longer we must both inevitably bring on the final crisis. Having already succeeded so well in my undertaking, I was anxious that she should enjoy the supreme happiness in the most complete manner possible, and I had little doubt that her excited passions would now induce her to give every facility to my proceedings. Changing her position a little to favour my object, I abandoned the advantage I enjoyed in the rear for the purpose of obtaining a more convenient lodgement in front. Inserting one knee under her thigh, I turned her over on her back, and throwing myself upon her to prevent her from rising, though to tell the truth, she did not appear to dislike the change of posture, I again tickled her up with my finger for a minute or two. Then withdrawing it from the delicious cavity and pressing her closely to my bosom and stifling her remonstrances with kisses and caresses, I endeavoured to replace the fortunate finger with the more appropriate organ, which was now fierce with desire, and burning to attain its proper position and deposit its luscious treasures within the delicious receptacle. The head was already at the entrance, and I was just flattering myself that another push or two would attain my object and complete our mutual happiness, when a confounded bell rang out loudly.

I at once foreboded that it sounded the knell of all my

hopes, for that opportunity at least, nor was I far wrong. However, I took no notice of it, but continued my efforts to effect the much desired penetration. But starting up with a strength and energy she had not previously exhibited, Eliza exclaimed, 'Oh, Sir Francis, you must let me go! It is the visitor's bell, and we shall be wanted immediately.'

I was extremely loth to lose the opportunity, and at first was disposed to try to retain the advantage I had already gained until I had secured the victory. But the evident distress she displayed affected me. I could not help feeling from the sudden change in her manner that it was urgent necessity, and not want of inclination, that forced her to put a stop to our proceedings. When she exclaimed, 'Oh, do have mercy on us! Think what would be the consequence if we were to be found in this state!' I could not resist the appeal, and allowing her to rise, I said that however greatly disappointed I might be at such an untoward termination to our amusements, I could not think of putting any contemplated enjoyment on my own part in competition with what might prove injurious to her, and that I should made no opposition to their leaving us at once, trusting that I should meet with the reward for my forbearance on some future more favourable occasion.

She thanked me warmly, and would doubtless have promised anything in order to get away, but I was not disposed to place much value upon any promises made in such a situation, and therefore did not attempt to extort any. She hastily began to arrange her dress, which had been not a little disarranged in the amorous struggle, and we then turned our glances towards George and Maria.

Whether it was that he had been more enterprising than I had been, or had met with less opposition. I know not, but when our attention was drawn to them we found Maria extended on her back on the sofa, with her legs spread wide out, and her petticoats above her waist, and George, with his trousers down about his heels and his plump white posteriors exposed to view quite bare, extended on the top of her, his legs between hers, clasping her tightly round the waist, and planting fiery kisses upon her lips, which were returned with interest. His buttocks were moving up and down with fierce heaves, and he endeavoured to effect his object and obtain admission to the virgin fortress.

At first I thought he had been more successful that I had been, but on a closer inspection, I found he was still beating about the bush, and that his weapon was still wandering in wild and hurried movements around the entrance without having yet hit upon the right spot, or managed to get within the secluded avenue of pleasure. Eliza spoke to them without producing any effect, and I was obliged to lay my hand on George's shoulder, and make him listen while I explained to him the state of matters. His answer was 'Oh goodness, I can't stop now, I must get it in.'

At this moment another bell rang, which Eliza told me was a signal they were wanted. There was now no help for it. I was forced to remind George that we should not only ruin the girls, but also lose all chance of having any future enjoyment with them if we allowed ourselves to be surprised on this occasion. It was with difficulty I could persuade him to get up and permit Maria to rise. He wished to keep the girls until they promised to come back to us; but as the thing must be done, I thought the sooner the better, and I therefore opened the side door and enabled them to escape to their own room where they hastened to repair the disorder in their hair and dress, which might have led to suspicion. Fortunately they were able to accomplish this and to make their appearance in the drawing room without their absence having attracted attention.

George had managed to extort a promise from Maria that they would return when the visitors departed; but not putting much faith in this, we dressed ourselves and proceeded to join them, hoping that we might be able to induce them to give us another opportunity when they were left alone. In this, however, we were disappointed. Being obliged to attend some ladies to their carriage, we found on our return that the birds had flown, nor did they make their appearance again till dinner time.

We were greatly annoyed at this unfortunate issue of our first attempt, just when it was on the very point of complete success; more especially, as every effort we could make to persuade them to give us another opportunity to accomplish our object was unavailing. It is true that all restraint among us was now removed. They laughed and joked with us, and did not take amiss the minor liberties we sometimes contrived to take with their persons. Nay, they even seemed to enjoy the fun, when occasionally, on a safe opportunity, we would produce our inflamed weapons and exhibit them in the imposing condition which their presence never failed to produce, in order to try to tempt them and to excite them to comply with our desires. Occasionally they would even allow us to place their hands upon them and make them toy and play with them; but still they took good care never to accompany us alone to any place where our efforts might be successfully renewed to accomplish the great object of our wishes.

One very hot day we took our books to enjoy the fresh air under the shade of a tree on the lawn in the front of the Abbey. We were quite near enough the house to be visible from the window, and the place was so exposed that it was out of the question to think of attempting the full gratification of our desires.

Nevertheless, we were so far off that our proceedings could not be distinctly observed, and there were a few low shrubs around which entirely concealed the lower parts of our persons, but still not so high as to prevent us from easily discovering if anyone approached us.

There was thus a fair opportunity afforded us for indulging in minor species of amusement for which we might feel inclined. Our desires, kept constantly on the stretch as they had been, were too potent to permit us to let such an opportunity escape us. George's trousers were soon unbuttoned, and his beautiful article, starting out in all its glory, was placed in Maria's hand.

After a little pretended hesitation and bashfulness, she began to get excited and interested in the lovely object, twisting her fingers among the scanty curls which adorned its root and toying with the little balls puckered up beneath, all which were freely exposed to her inspection.

For my part, I had laid my head on Eliza's lap and, slipping my hand under her petticoats, had insinuated a finger within her delicious aperture, playing with it, and tickling it, in the most wanton manner I could devise. The effects of both these operations were soon quite apparent on the lovely girls. Their eyes sparkled, and their faces became flushed, and I had very little doubt that could it have been safely done, they would have consented to gratify our fondest desires. I knew that some visitors were expected to spend the afternoon with us, who would occupy the girls and prevent any chance of further amusement for that day at least; and it occurred to me that though it would be too rash to attempt the perfect consummation of our happiness, we might at least indulge ourselves by carrying our gratification as far as we could safely venture to do so, and at all events thoroughly enjoy all the minor pleasures which were within our power. I therefore made a sign to George, which he at once understood. Following my example and getting his finger within Maria's centre of pleasure, he operated upon it in such an agreeable manner that she became excited beyond measure. Stretching herself beside him, she convulsively grasped the ivory pillar which she held in her hand, hugging and squeezing it and indulging in every variety of tender pressure. George instantly took advantage of her excitement, and while he continued to move his finger rapidly in and out of her lovely grotto, he agitated his own body so as to make his throbbing member slip backwards and forwards in the fond grasp which she maintained upon it. His involuntary exclamations of rapture and delight appeared to touch and affect Maria, and seeing how much pleasure she was giving him, as well as receiving herself, she could not refrain from trying to do everything in her power to increase his enjoyment. A word or two from him, every now and then, regulated the rapidity of their movements, and I soon saw that they were on the high road to attain that degree of bliss to which alone we could aspire under present circumstances.

Finding them so well employed, I hastened to follow their example. Unloosening my trousers, I set at liberty my champion, which was burning with impatience to join in the sport. Taking Eliza's hand, I placed it upon the throbbing object. She started with surprise and pleasure, on feeling its hot inflamed state, but did not attempt to remove her hand from where I placed it. She was sitting on the ground, with her back leaning against a tree. I gently raised up her petticoats and, slipping my hand beneath them, separated her thighs, and pressed my lips upon her springy mount and kissed it fondly. Searching out with my finger the most sensitive part, I played with it and tickled it until it swelled out and became inflamed to the utmost degree.

I soon ascertained the successful effect of my operations by the delightful manner in which she rewarded me, compressing my organ of manhood in her charming grasp in the most delicious manner possible and meeting and humouring the hurried and frantic thrusts with which I made it move to and fro between her fingers.

Finding that she was quite willing to continue the operations, which afforded us both so much enjoyment, I raised myself up on my knees, and while I gazed in her lovely countenance, sparkling with all the fires of luxurious delight, I exhibited to her the full proportions of my foaming champion as it bounded up and down under the fierce excitement of the delicious pressure she exercised upon it. I had intended to have made her witness the final outburst of the tide of pleasure. And, therefore, while I kept up the pleasing irritation with my finger, I purposely delayed bringing on with her the final crisis. But as I felt the flood of rapture ready to pour from me, I could restrain myself no longer, and hastily drawing up her petticoats before she could make any opposition, I bent forward and threw myself down across her. My stiff and bursting instrument penetrated between her thighs, and deposited its boiling treasure at the very mouth of the abode of bliss. As the stream of pleasure continued to flow out from me in successive jets, I felt Eliza's body give a gentle shiver under me. We lay wrapt in bliss for some minutes, during which she made no attempt to dislodge me from my situation. I guessed what had happened to her; but to make certain, I again placed my finger within her aperture and found the interior quite moist with a liquid which I knew had not issued from me.

When I put the question to her, she acknowledged with burning blushes that from the excited state she had been in, the touch of my burning weapon so near the critical spot had applied the torch to the fuel ready to burst into flame, and had brought on with her the final bliss at the very same time with me.

As I wiped away the dewy effusion from her thighs, I tenderly reproached her with having allowed it to be wasted in such an unsatisfactory manner, when it might have afforded so much greater gratification to us both. I could read in the pleased and yet longing expression of her lovely eyes that such a consummation would have been no less agreeable to her than to me; and I could fancy that were a favourable opportunity to offer itself, there would now be no great objection to her part to allow the wondrous instrument of pleasure, on which she again gazed with surprise and admiration as it throbbed and beat in her fond grasp, to take the necessary measures to procure for us both the highest gratification of which human nature is susceptible.

On casting my eyes around to where George and Maria were placed, I saw that we were still in time to enjoy a delightful spectacle to which I hastened to call the attention of my companion. George was stretched at full length on his back on the ground. The front of his trousers was quite open, disclosing all the lower part of his belly and his thighs. His charming weapon protruded stiff and erect up from the few short curls which had begun to adorn it. Maria was kneeling astride of him, grasping in her hand the instrument of bliss, and urging her fingers up and down upon it with an impetuosity that betokened the fierce fire that was raging within her. George's operations upon her we could not discern, for his head was buried between her thighs, and was entirely concealed by her petticoats, which fell over it. But that he was employed on a similar operation was quite evident from the short hurried movements which her posteriors kept up, no doubt in response to the luxurious and provoking touches of his penetrating finger. Maria's face was bent down within a few inches of the object of her adoration, upon which she was too intent to take any notice of us.

We enjoyed for a minute or two the pleasing contemplation of her delightful occupation and of the libidinous heaves of George's buttocks, which increased in strength and rapidity as the critical moment began with him. At length it arrived, and accompanied with an exclamation of rapture, the creamy jet issued forth from him with an energy that made it fly up, and bedew the countenance of the astonished Maria. Retaining her grasp, she gazed for an instant with rapture on this unexpected phenomenon; but her time was to come too, and almost before George's tide had ceased to flow, she sank down upon him, pressing his still stiff and erect weapon to her lips, and showering kisses upon it while, as we soon found, she repaid George's exertions with a tender effusion from her own private resources, which somewhat calmed her senses and restored her to reason.

When we had a little recovered ourselves, the girls appeared to be rather ashamed of the excesses which they had committed. And as George continued to tease them not a little, regarding the sacrilege they had been guilty of in thus wastefully pouring out both their own and our treasures, they soon took refuge in the house to hide their blushes and confusion.

We soon found, however, that though still too frightened to allow us to proceed to the last extremity, they would have no objection to a renewal of our late exploit. But this did not suit the purpose of George and myself, and we were determined not to allow them thus to tantalize us and slip through our fingers, now that we had obtained such a hold over them.

After some days' fruitless endeavours to effect our object, we became aware that we must again resort to stratagem for success. But the difficulty was how to accomplish it, for after having been once entrapped, they were now upon their guard with us.

We had taken down with us some of the best amatory pictures we could procure, and on the night of the flogging scene, when we found we could not prevail on them to return with us to the library, George had told them that we were not going to imitate their cruelty but would do all in our power to amuse them, and that he would accordingly deposit the pictures in the old hiding place that they might inspect them whenever they felt disposed. We kept a watch upon them, but without any great hope of immediate success from the stratagem, as we were aware they would suspect us and would take care not to be caught looking at them. We soon discovered however, from the marks we placed, that they were in the habit of amusing themselves with those pictures when they were certain we were out of the way, and we laid our plans accordingly.

One morning it was announced at breakfast time that the old ladies were going to dine that day at the house of a friend some miles off, so that the young people would be left quite alone for the whole evening. Although we were perfectly aware of this, and had founded our scheme upon it, we affected not to have known it. George turning to me said, 'Oh Frank, this will suit us nicely. Mrs Montague will perhaps be good enough to allow us to dine at luncheon time, and by that hour the river will be in prime fishing order after the rain, and we shall have a good afternoon's sport.' Mrs Montague at once agreed and gave orders accordingly. I thought the young ladies looked rather blank at this announcement, and I told George to whisper to Maria that if they would promise to be kind to us, we would return at seven o'clock to take tea with them when we would have the house all to ourselves. This satisfied them and put them off their guard.

All proceeded as we hoped. After luncheon we started for the river, and plied our rods as effectually as we could, in order that we might have something to show on our return. When the time approached at which the old ladies were to leave the Abbey, we returned to it; and hiding our fishing apparatus in one of the plantations, we made our way into the library by the window which we had purposely left open. We then concealed ourselves in a large closet of which there were two, one on each side of the window. We knew we could accomplish this without discovery as the girls would then be engaged assisting the old ladies to dress.

Having safely ensconced ourselves in our hiding place, we waited patiently at first for the departure of the old people. In a short time the carriage came to the door, and soon after we heard it drive off. We now became very impatient, for we confidently trusted that the girls would take advantage of such a favourable opportunity of being left entirely to themselves to derive some amusement from an inspection of the pictures, to which George had told them the night before that he had added some new ones, and we had taken care that they should have no opportunity of looking at them that day. Imagine therefore our dismay when we heard them leave their own room, proceed to the front door, and issue forth, closing it after them somewhat loudly.

George was in a sad state of vexation, and proposed that we should follow them, but this I objected to, saying that we should have plenty of time if we were obliged to go to work openly, and it was well worth while to wait patiently for some time longer for the chance of taking them at such advantage as would place them entirely in our power. George acquiesced and agreed to remain quiet. But his patience had nearly forsaken him when he heard the side door, which gave access to the library from the garden, gently open. We were in a state of anxious suspense until we heard it close, and beheld Maria's face peep through the door of the library. Finding all apparently safe, she came into the room and was immediately followed by Eliza. They closed the door softly, and we at once anticipated complete success as soon as we saw them draw the bolts of both it and the principal door. Our impatience was now extreme, but seeing everything proceeding so favourably, so resolved to curb it until we were in a situation to make the most of the advantage we had calculated on gaining. We therefore remained perfectly quiet, watching their proceedings.

Apparently satisfied that there was no occasion for any restraint upon their actions, they threw off all disguise and, removing their bonnets, proceeded to open the secret place and take out the pictures. They inspected them for some minutes, evidently with great pleasure, and the luscious details of the libidinous scenes they saw there depicted soon produced their natural effect upon them. After some little preliminaries, Maria laid herself back at full length upon the sofa, stretching out her legs before her, and drew up her petticoats as far as they would go; and at the same time pulled up the petticoats of Eliza, who was sitting beside her turning over the pictures, in such a manner to exhibit her thighs, belly, and the beautiful cleft with its surrounding fringe of curly hair. She inserted a finger into it and proceeded to titillate it, while with her other hand, she operated a similar diversion on her own charming aperture.

This was too much for us to view, and stand longer inactive. We had quite divested ourselves of the whole of our clothes, and softly opening the door, we rushed out perfectly naked, and with splendidly erected weapons threw ourselves at once upon our defenceless prey. They were so utterly taken by surprise, and so confounded at the state in which we appeared before them and the situation in which they themselves had been discovered, that they were perfectly unable to stir, and remained motionless in the same attitudes until we had clasped them in our arms and pressed them to our breasts, without their having the power to make the slightest resistance.

Maria's position, stretched at full length on the sofa, with her legs hanging down and wide apart, was too tempting to be resisted. In an instant George was between her thighs, his arms clasped around her waist, his naked belly rubbing against hers, and his fiery champion pressed against the lower part of her belly, endeavouring to find an entrance to that abode of bliss from which he had just snatched her finger, with the intention to replace it with a more satisfactory and appropriate organ.

For my part, though equally desirous to profit by the occasion, I was still cool enough to decide upon the best course of procedure. There was only one sofa in the room, so that only one pair could, with comfort and satisfaction, proceed with the pleasing operation. George was so maddened with excitement that I saw he could brook no delay, and I resolved that I should allow him to accomplish without hindrance his first victory in the field of Venus. I was the more induced to do this from the consideration that the exploration my finger had already made on the former occasions had convinced me that the fortress I had to attack was to be approached by an entrance so straight and narrow that the passage of my battering ram into the breach was not likely to be effected without considerable difficulty, and some suffering on the part of the besieged party. From George's account, there was not likely to be the same difficulty with regard to Maria, partly because her entrance was more open and partly because his member had not yet attained the same size as mine.

All these considerations made me think it advisable to secure every advantage by having Eliza favourably placed in a convenient position on the sofa before I attempted the assault; and I thought likewise that the previous sight of the raptures, which I was certain George and Maria would experience and exhibit before her, would encourage her and reconcile her to any little suffering she might undergo in becoming qualified to enjoy a similar bliss. I therefore sat down on the sofa, and keeping her petticoats still raised up, I made Eliza sit down, with her naked bottom on my knees, and slipped my instrument between her thighs so as to make it rub against the lips of her lovely aperture. At the same time I whispered to her that I thought we had better allow George and Maria to enjoy themselves in the first place, as there was not room for us all on the sofa at the same time.

She was in such a state of confusion and distraction, arising from the shame of having been detected in her previous occupation, as well as from the exciting nature of the novel scene now presented before her eyes of two handsome youths exhibiting all their naked charms, that she was in no condition to resist anything I required. But wishing to keep up her excitement to the utmost, I now directed her attention to the proceedings of our companions.

Maria apparently now thought that it was no use to mince matters, and that as the operation must be gone through, she might as well enjoy it thoroughly. Accordingly, instead of making any resistance, she had clasped her arms round George's naked body, and with burning kisses was animating him to his task, while the forward movements of her buttocks to meet his thrusts, showed that her anxiety was fully equal to his that they should effect an immediate and pleasing conjunction. I saw, however, that in their inexperience they were still beating about the bush, and had not yet taken the proper means to introduce the impatient stallion into the opening that was thus left quite free for his reception. I said to George, 'Wait a minute, my boy, I think I could manage to place you in a more satisfactory position.'

Throwing my arms round the legs of both, I lifted them up and placed them in an advantageous position on the sofa. Then inserting my hand between their bellies, I laid hold of George's fiery weapon, and keeping it directed right upon the proper spot, I told him to thrust away now. This he did with hearty good will. The first thrust he was within the lips, the second he was half way in, and the third he was so fairly engulfed, that I had to let go my hold, and withdraw my hand, so as to admit of their perfect conjunction.

At the first thrust Maria met him with a bound of her buttocks, at the second she uttered a scream, and as he

41

penetrated her interior at the third, she beseeched him to stop, saying that he was killing her. George, however, was not now in a state to be able to listen to her remonstrances. Satisfied that the worst was over and his object fully gained, as much to her benefit as his own, he merely replied with repeated fierce heaves and thrusts, while his fiery kisses seemed intended to stifle her complaints. A very few movements of his weapon, driven in as it was from point to hilt within her, were sufficient to drown all sense of suffering, and to rekindle the flame of desire which had previously animated her. Very soon her impetuous and lascivious motions rivalled his own in force and activity, as straining each other in their close embrace they strove to drive the newly-inserted wedge still further and further into the abode of bliss. Maria's upward heaves and the impetuous motions of George's bounding buttocks, as they kept time together at each luscious thrust, soon produced their pleasing effect, and with a cry of rapture, the enamoured boy, drowned in a sea of delight, poured forth his blissful treasures, while the no less enchanted girl, wrought up to an equal pitch of boundless pleasure, responded to his maiden tribute by shedding forth the first effusion ever drawn from her by manly vigour, a happy consummation which was accompanied on both sides with the most lively demonstrations of perfect delight.

While they were thus so agreeably occupied, I had been almost as much so in watching the effect which this luxurious scene produced upon Eliza, and in doing all in my power, by directing her attention to the various symptom's of enjoyment they exhibited and by caressing and toying with her in the most luxurious manner I could devise, in order to prepare her fully for following out the good example set before us. I had determined, if possible, to add to my pleasure by reducing her to the same state of nature in which I was myself. At first she objected to my removing her clothes. But soon getting excited with observing the wanton proceedings of George and Maria, as was clearly evinced to me by the tender squeezes she gave to my

42

sensitive plant, which I insisted on her holding in her hand, she ceased to make any opposition to my proceedings. I therefore managed to remove her stays, and to loosen all the fastenings of her dress, so that her petticoats hung loosely about her.

While George and Maria lay motionless in the blissful trance which follows the thorough completion of our fondest desires, I made Eliza rise from my knee, on which her petticoats slipped down, leaving her nothing but her chemise as a covering. This I also attempted to remove, but she insisted on being allowed to retain this last protection to her maiden modesty.

George, immediately on recovering his senses, started up and, disengaging himself from Maria, exhibited to us his conquering weapon, still erect and covered with semen slightly tinged with the gory marks of his triumphant success. On seeing the state of matters, and divining my object, he exclaimed, 'Oh, this will be capital; it will be such fun to see you two at it naked.'

Coming to my assistance, he occupied Eliza's attention by threatening an attack upon her still virgin citadel, under cover of which I had no difficulty in slipping her chemise over her head.

Intent upon now accomplishing the desired object, I clasped her naked form in my arms, and pressed my glowing body against hers with all the ardour of youthful desire. George assisted Maria to rise from the sofa, which was no sooner left vacant than I laid my not unwilling partner upon it, and separating her thighs, got between them and applied love's arrow to the appropriate mark.

Seeing that I was on the point of commencing operations, George said to Maria, 'Come, let us try if we can't give him a little of the kind assistance he rendered us. I shall keep the lips open while you shall hold the rudder in its proper place.'

Presently I felt the mouth of the opening distended, making way for the point of my weapon to press forward, while Maria's left hand pressed the shaft and tickled the

43

depending balls. I then heard Maria say, 'What is the reason, George, that yours is not so big as this?'

'Never do you mind!' was his reply; 'it is quite big enough for you, as you found not long ago, and it will be as big as his when I am as old as he is.'

'You are quite right, my dear fellow,' said I. 'I don't think mine was as big as yours is now when I was your age. And it was just as well for Maria that it is not bigger, as it has saved her some of the pain which I am afraid I must inflict upon my little darling here, before we can enjoy the same pleasure you have done; but I am sure she will believe me when I tell her that I shall spare her as much as I possibly can, and that it will be nothing compared with the pleasure she will enjoy when we are once fairly united.'

'Oh, I shan't pity her at all!' said Maria. 'I am sure I would suffer ten times as much as I did, most willingly, for the same pleasure.'

I was meanwhile proceeding with the operation as satisfactorily as I could expect. George and Maria performed their parts capitally and kept everything in due order, so that I had merely to press forward, which I did as rapidly as I could venture upon in the circumstances. I found the entrance as narrow and as difficult to force as I had anticipated, but the obstructions gradually gave way before the steady pressure forwards which I applied, until I had reached nearly half way in. Then I was forced to come to a stop for a moment, while I endeavoured to pacify her struggles and soothe her anguish, by assuring her that it would soon be over, and she would be made perfectly happy. I felt, however, that a vigorous effort must still be made to achieve the final victory; and the swollen and almost bursting state of my virile member gave me warning that unless this effort was speedily made, the opportunity might be lost for the present at least.

Satisfied that it was better for my companion to have the worst over at once, I kissed her fondly, and straining her to my body with all my power, I pushed forward with a steady pressure, driving on my fiery steed with all the impetus I

could give him, till he fairly burst the opposing b
forced his triumphant way into her inmost recess

I had no sooner done so than the warm flesh of
recess closing around the entire circumferenc
intruding member in the most delicious manner, forced the
tide of joy to burst from me. I sank upon her bosom in the
height of bliss, while the poor suffering girl, entirely
overcome with the pain of the sudden smart occasioned by
the opening up on this narrow passage, after giving vent to a
shriek wrung from her by the intense suffering, closed her
eyes and lay motionless under me, as if she had fainted.

When the first overpowering sensations of intense bliss
had subsided a little, I endeavoured to recall the swooning
girl to her senses, and the first sharp pang of agony having
passed away, she soon showed symptoms of recovery.
Thinking that the only way to recompense her for her
suffering, was to make her, as speedily as possible, partake
in the raptures she had afforded me, I ventured to move
gently once or twice backwards and forwards within her;
the first time I did so, she winced again and with difficulty
suppressed a scream; but after two or three repetitions
performed in a slow and gentle manner, she acknowledged
that the intruder no longer hurt her.

Encouraged by this, I was proceeding more vigorously;
when George, seeing that I was fully intent on running a
second course, exclaimed, 'Come, come, this is not fair; it is
our turn now.'

'No, no, my dear boy,' replied I, 'you had the first
opportunity, and it is only fair that we should begin first this
time; besides Eliza has had no enjoyment yet, and I am
afraid that after what has suffered, she will never allow me
to get in again, if I let her off without making her fully
sensible of all the pleasure her new acquaintance can give
her now that he is fairly lodged in the proper quarter.'

'Well, well,' replied he, 'go on, only make haste, for
Maria is tickling me up at such a rate that I am afraid she
will make me part with my treasure too soon, without being
able to give her the benefit of it.'

. did not require any further stimulus to urge me on in the path of pleasure. The whole lascivious scene we had gone through, and the tight pressure which the virgin sheath exerted upon my burning priapus, excited my lustful propensities to the utmost, so that even my recent effusion had hardly perceptibly diminished my vigorous powers. Gradually increasing the force and velocity of my thrusts, I worked away up and down in the narrow receptacle, which, now lubricated by my plentiful emission, afforded an easier passage for the delighted member which was procuring us so much pleasure. I had very soon the satisfaction of finding that his operations were not only harmless, but that they even seemed to afford delight to my darling girl. By degrees, her embrace round me was tightened, her lips returned my luxurious pressures, her buttocks began to heave in unison with mine; at first keeping pace with the movements, but soon agitating themselves up and down in a still more rapid and lascivious manner.

Observing these symptoms of the approach of pleasure, I redoubled my efforts and quickened my motions, so as to accelerate the progress of the internal operation, and just as I felt the second tide of rapture bursting from me, she uttered a cry – not this time the signal of pain, but of the most extreme delight; and after a prolonged upward heave, as if she wished to ram still more and more of the pleasure giver within her, she sank back on the sofa in the utmost ecstasy, enjoying to the fullest extent the blissful delight of the first complete sexual enjoyment she had ever tasted.

She remained so long in the agony of pleasure that I was able gradually to withdraw the instrument of her martyrdom and of her delight, and to wipe away the mingled stream of blood and semen which followed its removal, before she was conscious of my proceedings.

It was fortunate that the scene of operations was covered with crimson leather, so that no stain was left upon it, or we should probably have got into a bad scrape.

George and Maria were too intent upon a renewal of their amusement, to allow her any longer repose. Seeing their impatience to begin again, I hastily raised Eliza in my arms and, placing her upon my knee, sat down to witness the repetition of the deed they had already performed. Taking a hint from our proceedings, George had by this time stripped Maria entirely naked. On this occasion they required no assistance in the operation. Maria herself guided George's weapon to the mark, and he no sooner found the lips parting, than bending forward with ecstatic delight, he penetrated her interior with one thrust, and never ceased his exertions till their mutual exclamations of satisfaction and delight showed that this encounter had not fallen short of the last in point of rapture and bliss.

While they ran their second amorous course, Eliza's curious hand was easily induced to occupy itself with caressing the strange machine which had just afforded her so much pleasure. A few touches and wanton pressures suffice to make it regain its former state of vigour and erection. Although at first she declared she was afraid to permit it again to enter within her now no longer virgin recess, she was soon persuaded to allow me to make the attempt, and by a little management and address I contrived to satisfy her that it could now make its way within and renew all her pleasurable sensations without any risk of a repetition of the so much dreaded first painful impressions. Protruding up between her thighs, and its coral head nestled within the charming recess, the wicked little monster remained quiescent during the remainder of George's engagement with Maria, the exciting scene making him occasionally give a bound upwards, till he was quite engulfed. No sooner were they induced to quit the post of pleasure, than without loosening the pleasant tie which bound us together, I placed Eliza again on the sofa, and afforded her a pleasing repetition of our former enjoyment. This delighted her even more than the last; for being unaccompanied by the slightest tinge of pain, she was enabled fully to enjoy all the blissful and maddening sensations which her new acquaintance was calculated to confer upon her, while stirring up the seeds of joy in her

47

sensitive region.

A third encounter was satisfactorily concluded by both sets of combatants with unabated delight. After this, the girls declared that they must leave us, as their longer absence would be noticed by the servants. Though unwilling to part from them, we were not much disposed to object to this, as we were both beginning to feel that a slight respite would be necessary to enable us to carry on the war with satisfactory vigour. And we still anticipated an opportunity for further amusement before the time the old ladies should arrive. We therefore allowed them to go; and after regaining our fishing apparatus, made our appearance as if just returned from the river and repaired to our rooms to change our dress.

When we entered the drawing room we found the preparations for tea all ready on the table, and the girls waiting for us. We had a good laugh at the awkward manner in which they moved across the room to the tea table, which plainly showed that our pastimes, however pleasing, had still left some remains of stiffness, which we at once declared nothing but a repetition of the same exercise would remove. As a matter of course I devoted myself to Eliza, who was busy making tea, leaving George to entertain Maria, which he proceeded to do in the most agreeable manner. My back was turned to them, and I did not observe what they were about till my attention was called to their operations by observing the colour coming and going on Eliza's cheeks, and the evident confusion she was in. Turning round, what should I find but the young rogue stretched out at full length on an easy chair, with his legs extended before him, and his trousers down at his heels, while Maria, with her petticoats tucked up round her waist, was seated astride him, impaled upon the pleasant stake with which she had recently renewed her acquaintance and which, stiff and erect as ever, again penetrated her vitals.

I at once exclaimed against this proceeding as running such a risk of discovery, but I found the young libertine was more prudent than I gave him credit for; and had already ascertained from Maria that he was quite safe. It appeared that there was a party at one of the farmer's houses that evening, and some of the female servants had applied to their young mistresses for leave to go to it.

The girls saw clearly the advantage to be gained by having the coast clear for that evening, and willingly gave the desired permission, not only to those who applied for it, but also to the one who should have waited on us at tea, promising that they themselves would remove the tea things to the butler's pantry, the menservants having gone with their mistress. They only stipulated that they should return in time not to be missed.

Finding the opportunity so favourable, I lost no time in following the agreeable example they had set us, taking the precaution first to lock the door. Drawing another easy chair to the table, I stretched myself out on it in a similar manner, and pulled down my trousers till my manly weapon stood out along my belly uncovered and firm and erect. I then raised up Eliza's petticoats, and made her take up her position across me with a leg on each side. After a few caresses on both sides, taking hold of my weapon, I held it straight upright, at right angles to my belly, and applying it to the mark, made Eliza sink down gradually upon it, and make herself fast to me by the most charming bond, the key fitting into the lock in the most delicious manner possible.

When this was fairly accomplished, I allowed her to remain quiet in this position, and proceed with her tea making operations. We all found this an extremely agreeable arrangement; but before our first cup of tea was finished, it became very evident that sundry shoves and heaves which were given on both sides sadly interferred with the work of carrying the cup to the lips, and rendered it necessary that a certain operation of a different kind should be performed between another pair of lips, before the fair riders and their unruly steeds could satisfactorily indulge their tea drinking propensities.

A regular race then ensued to ascertain which of the two

couples should first reach the goal of pleasure, in which the fair jockeys exerted themselves with the utmost animation, and which ended in a dead heat.

The fire of the coursers having been somewhat tamed by this proceeding, they were allowed to remain quiet in their most agreeable stables until tea was concluded. By this time having again become mutinous, and lifting up their proud heads as if challenging another contest, their fair riders were no ways disinclined to afford them a further opportunity of distinguishing themselves in the course of pleasure. There was no occasion for whipping and spurring. Gently rising in the saddle, and then again sinking down, so as always to preserve their firm hold over their bounding steeds, they roused them up to the highest pitch of excitement and were amply rewarded for the pleasure they gave by the corresponding efforts which their animated proceedings drew from their generous steeds. I believe the contest ended by Eliza bringing in her dripping courser a short space in advance of her competitor; but all parties were so much overpowered by the delicious enjoyment which was the result of the struggle that they were hardly conscious of what was happening to one another.

Readjusting our clothes, and getting quit of the tea things, we then sat down for a short time to the piano, when a few songs of the warmest and most impassioned nature again set us agog, and necessitated another application of the cooling liniment to the wanton spot of pleasure. Our amorous pranks were, however, now put a stop to by the return of the old ladies. Warned by the sound of the carriage wheels on the gravel, we adjusted ourselves in proper positions and were found by them performing a very different sort of duet from that which had occupied the two couples all the previous part of the evening.

When the ladies arrived, we learnt, to our dismay, that the house was to be filled with company the following day. They had met with some friends, whose visit in the neighbourhood had been cut short by the dangerous illness of the lady in whose house they were residing, and it had been hastily arranged that the whole party should, in the meantime, take up their abode in the Abbey.

This greatly annoyed us; for all restraint being now banished from among us, we had calculated upon many a happy hour being spent in the library, which was hardly ever visited by the old ladies; and we sadly feared that the presence of so many visitors would prove a great hindrance – if it did not put a complete stop – to our pleasant intercourse.

But matters turned out more favourably than we anticipated and the very event we dreaded only tended to increase our happiness. At breakfast the next morning there was some discussion as to where the different visitors were to be accommodated, a difficulty arising in consequence of two of them requiring rooms on the ground floor, both being unable to mount upstairs with ease, the one from fat and the other from lameness. As our rooms were on that floor, we thought ourselves constrained to offer to vacate them; but fortunately they were not considered eligible, being though more suitable for gentlemen than ladies, from their being detached from the other sleeping apartments. The matter was arranged by the fat lady getting an unoccupied room and the lame one and her niece getting two adjoining apartments, which had hitherto been occupied by Miss Vivian and the young ladies. Miss Vivian took another apartment upstairs, and the girls were to occupy a room above the libary, which had formerly been used as their nursery.

I had been somewhat stuck with the peculiar construction of the building, of which I had taken some sketches, and had especially noticed one peculiarity – that all the rooms had two accesses, opening either into the passages or into the adjoining room.

On finding that the girls were to be separated from Miss Vivian, it occurred to me that it would be desirable to ascertain whether this peculiarity might not be turned to account so as to enable us to get access to our loves during the night, when alone we could hope to enjoy our mutual bliss in peace and safety. I therefore made them point out to me where their new habitation was to be; and on observing its locality, my hopes were greatly raised by what I discovered.

The main building of the house consisted of three sides of a square, along the interior of which ran a gallery on each floor looking inwards, so that all the rooms looked outwards. The library was in a sort of tower, at one angle, which was a storey higher than the rest of the building. There was a large unoccupied room above the library, and above that again were situated the nursery, as it was called, and another room. The principal entrance to those rooms above the libary had been closed up, and the only access at present to the nursery was by a winding staircase in a sort of turret at one corner of the tower. Our apartments were in a detached addition to the other side of the tower from this staircase, and at the angle which adjoined my room there was a similar turret, to which a door in my room appeared to open, but which was kept locked. I was in hopes there might be another staircase communicating with this door, and leading to the upper apartments.

I mentioned my idea to George, who was delighted with the prospect it held out. I told him that it would be very desirable if we could pay a visit to the girls' room, so as to discover exactly how matters stood and ascertain if there really was any communication by the turret adjoining my room. He said he could easily accomplish this, as I had not yet visited the haunted room, and he would apply for the key that he might show it to me.

The haunted room was the one immediately above the library. It was a large apartment, and at one time had been used as a sort of banqueting room, but had long been abandoned and shut up in consequence of a neighbouring proprietor having been killed in a drunken brawl, whose ghost was said still to haunt the room.

George contrived to arrange that the girls should accompany us in our exploration. We first proceeded to their room, and to our great delight, I was confirmed in my belief, by finding that the upper storey consisted of two rooms, apparently similar to each other, and having a door of communication, which, however, was locked. To my questions, the girls replied that in the other room there was also a door similar to the one which communicated with the turret in their room, and I had no doubt this door led to another staircase in the corresponding turret. I therefore determined to make any attempt at least to find our way from my room to theirs by this means.

Finding ourselves alone with the girls, we endeavoured to persuade them to allow us to satisfy the natural desires which their presence occasioned; but though they were strongly tempted by the potent arguments we produced to enforce our request, they were too much alarmed at the risk of being discovered with us in their room to allow us to proceed to extremities.

Respecting their fears, we desisted from our entreaties, and then descended to the haunted chamber, which must at one time have been a handsome room, but from which the furniture had been removed with the exception of some old tapestry and a few paintings on the panels. After examining these, we again fell to work caressing the girls when George said there could be no fear of being surprised there, as none of the servants dared enter that room and the old ladies were too much occupied with making the necessary arrangements for their guests to think of coming there. The girls admitted that this was the case, but stated the difficulty that, as there was no furniture in the room, they would have to lie down on the floor, which would be sure to soil their dresses and lead to suspicion.

On looking round the room, I saw that the only article it contained was a large heavy stand for flowers, which, however, I thought might be made to answer our purpose. Telling George to lock the door, and take out the key, I took hold of Eliza, and made her lean her hands upon the stand, and bend forwards, so as to make her posteriors project. Then turning up her petticoats over her back, I exposed her beautiful white buttocks to the light. Kneeling down, I pressed my lips upon them, and inserting my face between her thighs, I kissed her beautiful mount, while I hastily unloosened my trousers, and tucking up my shirt, exposed my erect priapus and prepared for an assault. Regaining a standing position, I spread her thighs asunder, and taking my place between them, I introduced my weapon from behind, between her lovely buttocks and, putting my hand in front, distended the lips of her charming cleft, so as to enable me to insert the point. This was no sooner accomplished, than by a few fierce shoves, I easily satisfied her that our object could be perfectly attained in this manner, by effecting the insertion of the whole of my weapon in her delightful receptacle, until my balls knocked against her thighs and our flesh was brought into the most delightful contact. My thrusts forward were soon responded to by her impetuous heaves backwards, and the delicious wriggle of her splendid bottom roused me up to an excess of furious delight.

George and Maria lost no time in following our example, and established themselves in a similar position on the opposite side of the stand, so that we could watch each other's proceedings. The stand was hollow in the centre, with nothing to intercept the view, and while engaged in the same process it was a lovely sight to behold Maria's white belly and the upper part of her beautiful little cleft surrounded with its mossy border, with the white shaft of George's weapon appearing and disappearing through the curly fringe, as he drove it backwards and forwards into the sheath of pleasure. Our impassioned heaves and struggles soon produced their usual luxurious effect, and we had to grasp our partners tightly around the middle, to prevent them from giving way under the delicious effects of the melting stream which we poured into them, and to which they responded with the utmost delight.

Uncertain when we might have another opportunity for a similar enjoyment, we insisted on retaining our positions for a second round of pleasure, and we met with but faint opposition from our not yet satisfied companions. The delight they enjoyed was excessive on finding the introduction of their pleasing favourite no longer attended with any symptoms of discomfort, and producing a superlative degree of pleasure far beyond the utmost they had ever anticipated. They both did everything in their power to render not only their own, but also our happiness as complete as possible, and we had every reason to be satisfied with the manner in which they entered into the spirit of the sport and forwarded our exertions to produce our mutual delight. Our frantic heaves and throbs were received and returned with equally voluptuous and pleasure-conferring shoves and wriggles, which gradually increased in force and intensity, until the final crisis again overtook us, and we all melted away in the glorious excess of rapture.

Our fair friends were then obliged to leave us to attend to the preparations for the visitors, and I repaired to my own room to try whether I could not manage to open up a communication between it and their new sleeping place, which we now desired to make the scene of our future revels; but no effort I could make with anything in the shape of a turnscrew which my gun-case afforded, or anything I could convert into a picklock, had the slightest effect on the obstinate lock of the door, which I supposed led in the wished for direction.

Determined not to give up the project without making a fair trial, I mounted my horse, and proceeded to a small town a few miles from the Abbey, where I procured a stout turnscrew, a few picklocks, a little wax and oil, and a dark lantern, which I resolved to make use of as soon as I had an opportunity.

The experience of the first day was sufficient to convince us that, as we had feared, the presence of the visitors prevented us from seeing almost anything of our young friends in private, and our anxiety was redoubled to procure an opportunity for meeting them quietly during the night.

As soon as the other inmates of the house had retired to rest, I set to work with the picklocks, but my skill with the burglars' instruments proved very limited, and I could not succeed in opening the lock of the first door. Fortunately it was an old-fashioned one, merely fastened on with screw nails on the side next me; and I soon managed to extract the screws and remove the lock. To our great satisfaction we found that the door led, as we expected, to a small staircase, similar to that at the other corner of the tower. With the assistance of the dark lantern, we then ascertained that there were also doors of communication with the library and the haunted chamber, and ascending higher up, we found another door, which we had no doubt must communicate with the room adjoining that occupied by the girls. On the lock of this door we exerted our utmost efforts for upwards of an hour, without success. It resisted every attempt we made to pick it, and the lock being fastened on the inside we could not remove it. At length it occurred to me that the locks of both doors were probably similar, and returning down stairs, I took to pieces the one I had removed and examined its construction. I soon ascertained the manner in which it worked, and found that by a slight alteration in one of the picklocks I could easily open it. Returning to the other door, I practised the same movement upon it, and very soon succeeded in forcing back the bolt. To our infinite satisfaction we found ourselves in the apartment next that of the girls, and discovered under the door of communication, a sheet of white paper, which we had told them to place there if all was safe for us to proceed with our enterprise. As I was required to take off this lock at any rate, I lost no time in attempting to pick it but at once unscrewed the nails, and in a few minutes we found ourselves in the presence of our charmers, who were safely ensconced in bed and waiting in anxious suspense for the accomplishment of our labours, the partial success of which they had discovered from the noise we made in removing the last lock.

Eager as we were to rush into their arms, we were still obliged to submit to a short delay, for, owing to the passage having been long closed up, the operations we had been engaged in had covered our persons with so much dust and dirt that we should have left behind us unpleasant tokens of our presence had we ventured to touch either our fair friends or the snow-white linen in which they were enveloped. Telling them the reason which occasioned this unpleasant delay, we hastily retreated to our rooms and performed our ablutions, taking the opportunity at the same time to remove our habiliments; and we returned upstairs merely in our shirts and dressing gowns.

As soon as we reached their rooms, even these garments were laid aside, and naked as the moment we came into the world, we jumped into the large bed which contained our charmers, and strained them in our loving arms.

After a storm of kisses and caresses, which were mutually lavished on all sides, we proceeded to disencumber them from all useless coverings, in order that we might enjoy in perfection the reward of our labours.

This was very soon accomplished, and the shutters being closed carefully and the curtains drawn so as to prevent the light betraying us, we lighted some additional candles we had provided, and hastened to avail ourselves of the rights we had earned by our exertions and which were most willingly conceded to us.

We were too impatient to spend much time in admiring the beauties which were freely exposed to our gaze, but mounting on top of our respective fair ones, we at once plunged our weapons into the well-fitting scabbards and proceeded to urge on our chargers at a furious rate. The rapidity of this operation soon produced a copious discharge on all sides.

A littled cooled by this, we disengaged ourselves from our sweet bonds, and devoted some time to an attentive survey of all those beauties of which we had now obtained full possession. Every portion of their bodies was passed under review, and each lovely charm drew forth our earnest commendations and was subjected to the warmest and most lascivious caresses. Nor did we, in our turn, escape from the same searching examination.

Maria's curiosity was openly displayed, and a little

encouragement soon induced her, and even Eliza, to pursue their researches until they had fairly investigated and thoroughly understood the mechanism of all those secret parts, the nature of which is generally so very carefully attempted to be hid from young ladies.

We agreed that by way of heightening the pleasure we should now join in the amorous encounter by turns, and endeavour mutually to add to each other's enjoyment during the process. Eliza and I were the first to commence. I again got upon her, and fixed my weapon in the sheath. I then made Maria place herself on her knees, with her legs astride Maria's head, so that during the whole operation my face was in close contact with her beautiful mount, while I kissed and caressed all her lovely charms. Making George kneel on the bed beside us, I placed Eliza's hand upon his rampant hero and made her play with the dependent jewels, until the agony of pleasure came upon her and drove everything else from her thoughts, forcing her to abandon even that pleasing amusement.

I was so excited with this lustful proceeding that finding my vigour still sufficient for another encounter, I could not make up my mind to quit such pleasing quarters as long as I could retain possession of them. Merely ceasing my active operations during the process of emission, I thrust away again with renewed earnestness and force, until I again brought my darling companion, as well as myself, to undergo the delightful sensations of a joint overflow.

On my withdrawing from my delicious position, George took his place on top of Maria and, transfixing her with his lance of pleasure, proceeded to follow our example. Observing that my worn-out charger bore evident marks of exhaustion from his continued exertions, and knowing that I had little time to spare that night for such pleasing enjoyments, he declared that he must try what he could do to re-animate its forces.

He therefore made me kneel in front of him across Maria's head, in the same way as she had done over Eliza, and as he proceeded with his lascivious course of heaves in and out of the cavity of his charmer, he took the point of my weapon in his mouth. Eliza was made to kneel beside me. With one hand he tickled Eliza's wanton gap with such address and vigour as to cause her to shed tears of joy. With the other he pressed and fondled the somewhat relaxed pillar of my sensitive member, making as much of it as possible enter his mouth and closing his lips upon it with a most delicious suction. Beneath, I felt the lips of the wanton Maria pressed fondly against the firm cheeks of my glowing buttocks, while her fingers tickled and played with the soft slippery balls which dangled down before her.

The effect of this voluptuous excitement was so great, that by the time George and Maria melted away in the sweet delirium of satisfied enjoyment, I was again in a position to renew the combat with Eliza, whose ardour, instead of being appeased, had only been still further excited by George's tantalizing substitute for my now renovated weapon.

After having acquitted myself to our mutual satisfaction in this final encounter, which, though longer, was not less sweet than any of its predecessors, I was forced reluctantly to tear myself away from their embraces, in order that I might proceed with the necessary operations to secure our safe meetings on future occasions.

George was preparing, though with equal reluctance, to accompany me, but I told him that one could now do all that was requisite and that there was no occasion to spoil his sport unnecessarily. The delighted boy, with many thanks, agreed to the proposal that he should remain where he was.

The next morning with tears of joy he thanked me for the happiness he had enjoyed and described how well he had employed his time; in proof of it exhibiting and making me feel the condition of his limp and worn-out weapon, which hung down its head in utter exhaustion; and declaring that he had spent the happiest night of his life, and that he could never hope to enjoy anything like it again.

While he was thus amusing himself, I dressed myself and proceeded to open the different locks, and take impressions in wax of them, in order that I might get keys made to fit.

Although we were obliged for a few days to content ourselves with fastening the doors with the bolts, trusting that they would not be examined, I was resolved not to run the risk of any suspicion being excited by their being found open at any future period. I then carefully oiled the locks, and replaced them.

By this time it was broad daylight, and I was forced to rouse George out of the fast slumber into which fatigue and exhaustion had thrown the lovely trio.

Without disturbing our fair partners, we returned to our own rooms, where I endeavoured to obtain an hour or two of sleep to recruit myself after all my labours.

That forenoon I carried the casts of the locks to a locksmith in the neighbourhood, whose acquaintance I had made while fishing in the river and whose good will I had secured by furnishing him with some flies, by virtue of which I had managed on more than one occasion to outstrip him in the sport and thereby endanger his reputation as the acknowledged champion of the river. I easily blinded him by making mysterious allusions to the servant maids, and in a couple of days I was in possession of keys which opened all the doors between our apartments. By means of these we every night proceeded to enjoy ourselves in the arms of our charmers, and retreated in the morning, fastening all the doors behind us, so that no shadow of suspicion was ever excited.

During the ensuing month, we indulged ourselves to the utmost, and varied our amusements in every way in which our excited imaginations could devise expedients for carrying our our frolicsome sports.

Before long it was quite evident that George was most anxious to have a little variety by entering the lists with Eliza, and also that Maria was very much inclined to try the effect of the introduction of my larger machine into her narrow slit. I was not so certain whether Eliza was willing to give up her rights over me, even for the sake of a taste of the enjoyment which could be afforded by the old acquaintance of her childhood. But after I had on several occasions made her admire its beauty and the delightful effects its produced upon Maria, I thought she was sufficiently interested in it to venture upon bringing out an exchange of partners.

I therefore one day taxed George with his inclination to taste the sweets of enjoyment with the more fully developed person of Eliza. He frankly acknowledged his wish, and said that nothing but the fear that it might be disagreeable to me had prevented him from proposing it, adding that he was quite sure Maria was just as much disposed for the change as he was as she had often expressed her enthusiastic admiration of my weapon.

I assured him that he would meet with no objection on my part, especially as he was fully entitled to enjoy all the fruits of his labour, for it was he who had originated and brought about the whole affair. I told him that if he could gain Eliza's consent, which I had little doubt of his easily obtaining, the sooner his wish was carried into effect the better.

He undertook to arrange matters with Eliza, and said he thought he would be able to manage it without compromising me in case of any objection on her part.

We were in the habit of sometimes making an exchange of beds, one of us remaining in the girls' room, while the other couple repaired to one of our rooms to pass the night.

One evening George and I were out at dinner at a residence in the neighbourhood, and did not return till after the remainder of the family had retired to rest. George told me to go to bed, and that he would send me a pleasant companion. I suspected from the way he spoke that he meant mischief, but I did as I was bid, and having undressed myself, I took my place between the sheets. In a short time I heard a light step in the room. George had extinguished the candle, and the person approached the bed and slipped into it without speaking. I was at once aware that it was not my usual bedfellow, but having no objection to the exchange, I was quite willing to encourage the frolic. At the same time I thought it would add to the fun if I were merely to act the part of a passive subject of the experiment

61

and allow my fair seducer to carry out her freak in her own way.

Appearing therefore not to be aware of the change of partners, I said that I was tired and disposed to be lazy; and that if she was inclined for any amusement that night, she must help herself to it. At the same time I stretched myself out on my back, leaving my upright priapus at full liberty to be operated upon in any manner she might think proper. My companion immediately accepted the proposal, and turning up my shirt and her own chemise, placed herself upon my belly, kissing me fondly. She then took hold of my instrument, which was beating fiercely against her warm soft belly, and applied it to her cleft, holding it in an erect position, and bearing down upon it with all her might, endeavouring to make it penetrate into the proper quarter. All her efforts however were ineffectual to make it enter the narrow channel, for though George had not found much difficulty in forcing his way where her finger had often been before, the larger dimensions of my weapon required the passage to be considerably distended before it could enter. But the little monkey was determined if possible to effect her purpose, and proceeded to put in practice a device which George had suggested to her. Creeping out of bed, she made her way to my dressing case, and taking out the cold cream, she smeared her own secret part and my member with it, and then resumed her position, and endeavoured with all her might to force the stubborn instrument into her. She so far succeeded as to get the top inserted within the lips of the cavity; but her unaided efforts were quite unavailing to ram it home. After a long series of fruitless efforts, during which I was malicious enough to give her no assistance though her wanton fingerings drove me almost frantic with pleasure, she found it quite impossible of her own accord to effect her purpose. Exhausted and disappointed, she laid her head on my bosom, and ceasing her efforts, burst into a fit of tears.

This was more than I could stand. So saying gently to her, 'You seem to be very awkward about it tonight, my darling; I suppose I must come to your assistance,' I threw my arms round her waist, and without disturbing the close contact of our bodies, I gently turned her over upon her back, assuming myself the position she had formerly occupied. The instant she was aware of my purpose, all her energy and desire seemed to recur in full force, and clasping me tightly in her arms, she twisted her legs round mine, so as to hold us firmly together and retain the slight advantage she had already gained of the partial introduction of my stretcher within the approaches to her seat of pleasure. When I found myself fairly established upon her, I had nothing to do but to force my way forward, which I proceeded to accomplish as effectually as possible. Notwithstanding the repeated inroads which George had already made within her territories, I found it no easy matter to effect a complete penetration. Her toying and playing with it and her endeavours to accomplish her object had excited and irritated my organ of pleasure to such a degree, that I could no longer restrain him from pouring forth his treasures, and I shot into the confined entrance a shower of boiling liquid.

On feeling the warm effusion issue from me without her being able to make a corresponding return, she uttered a low exclamation of disappointment and regret. As soon as the pleasure fit was over, I hastened to make up to her for the loss she had sustained. Assisted by the lubrication of the parts which this contretemps had effected, I no longer found the same difficulty as formerly, and I became sensible that I was fast slipping forwards and making progress in the accomplishment of the desired object. But if I was now satisfied with the state of affairs, poor Maria was no longer so; and she evidently was becoming convinced that the proceeding was to be, at first at least, a more serious undertaking than she had anticipated. Instead of as at the beginning meeting every heave and thrust I gave with a corresponding movement on her own part, she now hung back, and as I continued my victorious progress within her, she was fairly overcome with the suffering I occasioned her, and earnestly beseeched me to stop, exclaiming that I was killing her. But it was too late now for her to make any opposition. I was too far advanced and too greatly excited to think of yielding for a moment to her entreaties, nor do I believe she would have been pleased if I had done so. Replying to her expostulations as if I had only just now discovered the impositions she had played upon me, I said. 'No, no, if young ladies will come and ravish young gentlemen in.the dark, they must take the consequences; but don't be afraid, the work is over now.'

As I spoke I gave a final thrust, which sent me up to her very vitals, and rendered any further exertions on my part, or suffering on hers, quite unnecessary. As our bodies came into perfect contact, and she felt that my instrument had penetrated her to the utmost extent, she uttered an exclamation, but whether it was of joy or sorrow I could not discover; probably it was a mixture of both, but there certainly here sorrows ended.

I gave her a little respite, and lay quite still upon her without moving until she should be perfectly recovered from the effects of the first insertion. Gorged and crammed as she was with the dainty morsel, it could not remain long in its present situation without producing its usual effect of stirring up the passions to the highest pitch. A warm kiss and a fond pressure which she gave me, as I ventured to move my weapon gently backwards and forwards in its new sheath, showed me that I might safely venture to continue my pleasing progress to the height of enjoyment. Step by step as I kept up my regular succession of thrusts, the voluptuous excitement gradually grew fiercer and fiercer within her. She clasped me to her, imprinted burning kisses on my lips, and twined her limbs around me in all the lustful frenzy of passionate desire on the verge of fruition, till the vigorous working of my furious instrument brought matters to a crisis with her. Then relaxing her hold, she muttered a few inarticulate sounds of delight, and melted away in the pleasing agonies of perfect enjoyment; in which a few more delicious thrusts made me join with equal satisfaction and delight.

After resting for a short time to recover from our fatigues, I resumed my position within her, and gave her another equally satisfactory proof of the pleasure she was to derive from her change of companions, and with a short interval, I followed up my success with a third victory, after which, she begged for a little repose, and we soon sank into sweet slumber.

In the meantime George had been equally fortunate in his enterprise. On going to the girls' room, he had found Eliza sound asleep. After sending Maria down to me, he took his place beside his slumbering companion. He watched his opportunity to turn her gently on her back, and separated her thighs. Then kneeling over her between them, he arranged this weapon directly above the darling object he desired to enter into, and letting himself suddenly fall down upon her, he by one plunge drove himself into the inmost depths of the voluptuous cavity, and in an instant arrived at the summit of his wishes. Thus suddenly aroused from her sleep, Eliza in her confusion did not at first discover the imposition, and fancying that it was I who was thus invading her sanctuary, she responded to his lascivious caresses and entered eagerly into the pleasing sport. Something however in his mode of proceeding roused her suspicions, and inserting her hand between their bellies, she grasped his instrument with her fingers and then felt the accompanying playthings. She had been too much accustomed to handle and play with both our members, not to discover the deception; but George had acquitted himself so well and, making the best use of his time, had taken such effectual means to make the most of the advantage he had gained, that the voluptuous crisis was just coming upon her as she became sensible of the true state of matters. In such a situation it was impossible for her to make any resistance, even if she had wished to do so, and George fully accomplished his object of securing not only for himself, but for her also, such a voluptuous and rapturous outburst of the fountain of delight, that it was quite out of the question for any female to be otherwise than charmed with the performance. As he refused to give up the advantageous position he had secured and maintained his place, he worked away with unabated vigour until he had produced a second delicious effusion on both sides; he had little difficulty before the conclusion, in gaining not only her pardon, but her thanks for the exchange he had thus brought about. Indeed it turned out that Eliza's only objection had been the fear of my being offended, and as soon as she was satisfied on this point, she did not hesitate to own to him that she had been quite as anxious as he was that the two old playthings of their childhood should be thus brought into mutual contact now that they were capable of affording each other so much enjoyment. And she not only permitted, but encouraged and seconded, all his libidinous endeavours to forward their mutual bliss.

As soon as daylight appeared, George insisted on Eliza going down with him to my room, to ascertain how we had been employing ourselves. I heard him coming, and tossing off the bed clothes from us, I hastily drew Maria upon me, and impaled her upon my upright stake. Though she writhed a little at its first introduction into her, there was no longer the difficulty which she had found on the previous evening. As George and Eliza approached the bed, the first thing that met their view was her lovely posteriors heaving up and down with all the ecstacy and delight of unsated desire, while as her thighs were stretched wide apart over me, the pillar of my staff of life appeared and disappeared again between them every time she rose and sank upon it. This sight at once removed any feeling of restraint. It was quite evident to them that we had enjoyed the change as much as they had done, and they eagerly took up their position beside us, fondling and caressing all our secret charms and encouraging us in our voluptuous exertions.

As soon as our course was run, I insisted upon their affording us the same animating sight. George, who had been quite enchanted to find that Eliza's charming and elastic cavity afforded him quite as much delight as that of Maria, soon stripped off the scanty clothing which covered them. Then, taking up his position on the lovely girl, he plunged his beautiful weapon into her delightful grotto. No sooner had it reached the bottom than the mutual and continuous movements kept up on both sides clearly proved that their previous maneouvres had been equally satisfactory to both parties, and that the pleasing conjunction they had thus again brought about was producing the most rapturous effects upon their senses. The rapidity and vigour with which their operations were conducted soom brought on the happy crisis; and with outstretched limbs and quivering muscles, they sank in the blissful swoon of perfect and unalloyed happiness.

Nothing more could be required to complete our enjoyment beyond the perfect abandonment to the most luxurous delights of voluptuous pleasure to which this mutual interchange of partners enabled us to give ourselves up without the least restraint. There was not a lascivious fancy that entered into our imaginations which was not carried into execution on the instant. Night after night we revelled in all the delicious sweets of unbounded and thoroughly gratified voluptuousness with all the zest of youth and passion, excited to the utmost by the charms of the lovely objects of our adoration, until circumstances occured which rendered it necessary for us to admit other participators in our pleasant pastimes. I must now bring the new actors on the scene.

The Visitors to the Abbey

It is now time to bring on the stage some of the visitors to the Abbey; and I shall commence with the party, the announcement of whose visit occasioned us so much consternation, but whose actual arrival afforded us the means of so much amusement by rendering necessary the removal of Eliza and Maria to the apartment to which we found such convenient means of access.

The party in question consisted of three persons: Mrs Vickars, a very stout old lady, remarkable for nothing but her invincible propensity to fall asleep whenever she entered a carriage; Miss Vickars, her daughter, somewhat of a literary turn and fond of chess – probably the result of a confirmed lameness which prevented her from moving about, and last and least, though in my opinion the principal person in the group, Fanny Vickars, the granddaughter.

I should find it difficult to give any adequate description of Fanny. She was one of those girls who do not strike you forcibly at first sight, but who gain upon you, and in whom you discover more attractions the more you see of her and the better you become acquainted with her.

Her features were regular and pleasing; her form, though not on a large scale, was admirably proportioned; and there was a quiet grace about her every motion which was extremely seducing. Her whole demeanour was so soft and gentle, that one never suspected the latent fire of passion which was hidden beneath it. Indeed, we were all taken in at first and were somewhat afraid of her. I was the first to suspect the truth, and had there been no counter attraction in the way I should probably have much sooner come to an understanding with her, but I was so much occupied with

Eliza and Maria, who certainly gave us enough to do, that I was less disposed than I might otherwise have been to press matters with her. Besides, she slept in her aunt's room and was so constantly in attendance upon her, and her grandmother, that there would have been great difficulty in carrying on any intercourse with her, to say nothing of the jealousy which such a proceeding might have created with the other girls. A simple event, however, produced an impression in my favour which gradually led to pleasing results.

Owing to the infirmities of Mrs and Miss Vickars, the one from her great corpulency and the other from her lameness, they were prevented from taking almost any exercise except in a carriage, and they were in the habit of driving out almost every day. As Mrs Vickars invariably fell asleep before she had been in the carriage many minutes, and as Miss Vickars found it very dull work to sit so long by herself, Fanny always accompanied them and played chess with, or read to her aunt, in order to pass the time.

One day the old ladies had announced that they were not to drive out, and the girls had arranged that Fanny should accompany them on their ride, and make use of Maria's pony, who being a good horsewoman was to ride my horse. Fanny had said nothing of this arrangement to her relatives, wishing that one of the girls should mention it, which they had omitted to do.

In the course of the forenoon the old ladies changed their intention, and told Fanny to order the carriage and get ready to accompany them. I happened to be in the room at the time and saw Fanny's disappointment. However, she said nothing of the arrangement with the girls and went off to do as she had been told.

As soon as she was gone, I said that I was afraid the girls would be sadly disappointed at the change of plans, and mentioned what they had proposed to do, adding that if they could spare Fanny for that day, I should be very happy to take her place and accompany them on their drive.

To do the old people justice, they were not at all disposed

69

to treat Fanny harshly, but they had been so long accustomed to have all their wants humoured by her that it never occurred to them that her ideas of amusement and pleasure might not correspond with theirs. On this occasion they at once gave their consent that she should accompany the girls, and wished me also to join the party. However, I was rather desirous to get upon good terms with the old people, and insisted upon going with them. As I expected, Miss Vickars and I were left to a solitary tête-à-tête, the old lady falling fast asleep in a few minutes after we started; and I gained her good graces by losing, apparently with difficulty, a couple of games of chess.

We usually had a dance in the evening, and that night Fanny took an opportunity of thanking me in very warm terms for the kindness I had shown her, and expressed how much gratification she had enjoyed from her ride. We happened to be walking in the passage, refreshing ourselves with the cool air after our waltz, and my hand had not left its position round her waist. I was struck with the warmth with which she spoke, and I involuntarily drew her to me and pressed my lips to her cheek, saying how delighted I was at having been able to afford her any pleasure. There was no one beside us at the time, and rather to my surprise, she made no attempt to escape from my embrace.

Emboldened by this, I ventured to transfer my lips to her mouth, and was charmed to find an answering pressure and a response to the warm kisses I imprinted upon it. Someone approaching us at that moment, I was obliged to desist, but as she reverted to the subject, apparently for the purpose of covering her confusion, I rather added to it by whispering that I should be amply repaid for anything I could do for her by such a reward as I had just received.

My interference on this occasion proved useful in breaking the thraldom to which she had till now been subjected, and after this she was not always expected to be in attendance upon the old people and her wishes were occasionally consulted in their arrangements. Sometimes, too, one of the girls, or George or I, would volunteer to take her place during the daily drives, while she accompanied us on our rides.

In this manner our intimacy gradually increased. I could not be thus daily brought into contact with her without getting a better insight into her feelings, and I began to suspect that the occasional caresses I sometimes found an opportunity of bestowing upon her, either during our evening amusements, or when assisting her to mount or dismount from her pony were not at all disagreeable to her, and might perhaps with safety be pushed further, if a favourable opportunity should offer.

For some time, however, this did not occur, and I was unwilling to run any risk of disturbing the pleasant arrangements of our charming party of four, by hazarding any proceedings which might excite suspicion in any quarter. I therefore restricted myself to an occasional repetition of the first caresses, sometimes accompanied with a gentle pressure of her swelling bosom, or of her voluptuous, finely formed thighs.

While I was thus daily becoming more and more desirous of bringing matters to a crisis, other events occurred which rendered it most desirable that I should be enabled to insure a favourable termination to my wishes without longer delay. We learned that Mrs and Miss Vickars were soon to leave the Abbey for a time, in order to pay a visit to some other friends and, as it was not convenient that Fanny should accompany them there, it was proposed that she should remain at the Abbey.

Other visitors were expected to come in their place, who were to occupy the rooms presently inhabited by Fanny and her aunt, and Mrs Vivian had talked of putting Fanny into the empty room in the tower, adjoining the one which was made use of by Eliza and Maria.

This proposal threatened to disturb all our pleasant arrangements, and though it might be possible for us to continue our nightly meetings by giving Fanny the outer room, and making the girls occupy the inner one, still we could hardly hope to carry on our intercourse as formerly without her becoming aware of the state of matters. Besides this, we expected our young friend, Hamilton, to spend a few weeks with us, and it occurred to me that it would be very desirable if we could secure the co-operation of Fanny, and induce her, in conjunction with him, to join us in our voluptuous orgies.

While thus in a state of doubt and indecision, not knowing how to bring about what I desired, an event occurred which suggested a mode of accomplishing it. One morning George was required by his grandmother for some purpose or other, and having nothing better to do, I threw myself on a sofa in the parlour, where I very soon became interested in perusing the proceedings of a celebrated divorce case, which was fully reported in the columns of *The Times*. Eliza was seated at the table, with her back to me, drawing, and Fanny was sitting at the window on the opposite side of the room, engaged with some worsted work. While turning over the page of the paper, my eye caught the sight of Fanny reflected in a large mirror over the mantelpiece.

She was sitting motionless with her work in her hand, but with her eyes intently fixed upon me, and her face glowing like scarlet. I had very little doubt as to what had attracted her attention and caused her agitation.

I was quite aware that the exciting nature of the details of the case I was reading had roused up the little gentleman, who is the *primum mobile* in such affairs, and without whose interference and wicked pranks there would be no necessity for the employment of the gentlemen of the long robes and the whole machinery of the divorce court, but as there was no one in the room except Eliza and Fanny, I had not thought it at all necessary to put any restraint upon myself, or to attempt to conceal the little rogue's excited motions. I could not but be convinced that it was the manner in which the unruly member throbbed and attempted to raise up its head under my somewhat loose and thin trousers, which had attracted her attention, and which seemed almost to have paralysed her.

The idea instantly occurred to me of trying how far I could work upon her, and to what extent I could excite her passions, by giving her as if accidentally a somewhat better idea of the nature of the object which had evidently roused her curiosity. My face was entirely hidden from her by the newspaper, and as her back was turned to the mirror, she could have no idea that I was watching her in it. I therefore gradually changed my position slightly so as to enable me to present the object more favourably to her, and putting down my hand, as if accidentally, I arranged my trousers so as to give her a fair idea of the size and form of the article beneath them, which became still more inflamed and agitated by the very idea that it was under her inspection.

The effect of this seemed to redouble her interest and attention. Her eyes remained fixed upon it, and she drew back her head a little behind the curtain, so as to conceal her face from Eliza, if she should happen to look up.

This convinced me my stratagem was succeeding, and I determined to proceed still further. Moving myself about as if uneasy in my position, I tried as far as possible to exhibit the excited weapon, so as to develop its form and shape. Finding that her ardent gaze still continued to dwell upon it, I covered it with the newspaper, and putting my hand down, I unloosened the front buttons of my trousers and removed the swollen pillar from its position upon my thigh, making it stand up erect along my belly. Then tucking up my shirt, in order to give it free exit, I arranged my trousers, so as to conceal the fact that they were unbottoned, and withdrew the newspaper. When she saw me move, she cast her eyes down upon her work, but as soon as I again took up the paper, her glance was again turned to the object that seemed to have captivated her. I could plainly see an expression of disappointment when she noticed that the object no longer appeared where she had formerly observed it. This expression, however, soon disappeared when, pressing myself gradually forward, I made the naked head of my member slightly show itself through my trousers. The moment she caught sight of the ruby point, her neck and face became suffused with a still more brilliant colour, but after a hasty glance, she almost instantly withdrew her eyes and turned them to her work.

I thought she seemed to doubt for a moment whether the change of position was not premeditated on my part. However on finding that I continued quietly to peruse the paper, without seeming to be conscious of the exhibition I was making, she appeared to take courage and again renewed her inspection.

I waited for a few minutes, and then slowly made the stiff member protrude further forward until one half of it was exhibited beyond my trousers.

She continued to gaze on it as if fascinated with the sight of the charming object. I was just hesitating what further to do, and was trying to discover by what means I could manage to indulge her with a sight of the whole of the inflamed weapon without alarming her, when I heard steps in the lobby and a hand was laid on the door handle.

There was no time to be lost. It would not do to run the risk of being caught in such a situation, but I was determined not to lose the advantage I had gained and I resolved to show Fanny that I was perfectly aware of what she had been about, and of the interest she had taken in the object she had been surveying. I therefore dropped the newspaper so suddenly that she had not time to change her position or to withdraw her eyes, and they encountered mine fixed upon her.

The smile on my countenance made her aware of the trick I had played her. Covering her face with her hands, and letting her work fall, she burst into tears and hurried from the room. I was not quite prepared for this denouement, but I thought I would only make matters worse by any attempt to console her, I therefore resumed the perusal of my newspaper, buttoning up my trousers, so as to conceal the offending object. It was Maria who entered the room. She put some question to Fanny, who passed her without giving any answer. Surprised at seeing her in tears, Maria inquired of us what we had been doing to her to set her crying.

'Crying!' said Eliza. 'Impossible; nobody has moved or spoken a word for the last quarter of an hour. It has been quite a Quaker's meeting.'

But as Maria persisted, Eliza got up and followed Fanny to see what was the matter. Maria was not satisfied, and her quick eye catching a glimpse of the excited condition of my member, she at once suspected that Fanny's distress had some connection with its present condition, and said she was strongly of the opinion that I had been playing some tricks upon her. I, of course, denied this, and appealed to Eliza, who had returned without seeing Fanny, as she had taken refuge in her aunt's room, where she did not like to follow her.

Eliza confirmed my statement; but Maria, taking hold of my electric rod and convincing herself of the state in which it was, persisted in declaring that it must have had some share in the matter. I said it must have been by some secret sympathy then, for the width of the room had been between us all morning, and told her to read the newspaper where she would soon find an explanation of the cause of my excitement.

A few minutes sufficed to rouse her passions to an equal pitch with my own, and pulling out my weapon, she proceeded to caress it in a manner that proved she was determined to allay the irritation under which it laboured. I remonstrated, faintly I must own, for her caresses were anything but disagreeable, on the inprudence she was committing; but she still persisted, and she did not desist till Eliza interfered on seeing her raise up her petticoats, and seat herself upon me, with the evident intention of inserting the weapon in its proper sheath.

Eliza pointed out the folly of needlessly running such a risk of discovery, when she had such full opportunity of indulging herself at night. Maria was most unwillingly convinced of the necessity of deferring her enjoyment, but she vowed that if Eliza treated me so ill as to allow me to remain in such a state of excitement, she would take me under her own charge, when she would make certain that I should not be able to play such tricks again during the day.

We saw nothing of Fanny till she made her appearance with her aunt at lunch. Maria rather wickedly began to rally her, talking of electric rods, metallic tractors, secret sympathies, and employing all the jargon of the mesmerists. Fanny was sadly confused, and cast a reproachful look upon me, thinking that we had joined in a plot against her.

I could not resist the mute appeal and came to her assistance, turning the tables upon Maria, so that she had quite enough to do to defend herself. For this I was rewarded with a look from Fanny, which showed that she appreciated my motive.

In the evening Fanny sat down to the piano, and George and I waltzed with the girls. Under the pretext that the room was too warm, I opened the door and extended our course to the adjoining corridor. After a while I asked Eliza to relieve Fanny at the piano, and I made her waltz with me. I took her two or three times up and down the corridor, and then stopped at the extreme end where we were quite out of sight of the rest of the party. Retaining my hold of her hand, I placed it upon my member, which was standing stiffly erect along my thigh as she had seen it in the morning. She struggled and tried to remove her hand, but I retained it, saying 'Fanny, my darling, you surely can't have any objection to becoming better acquainted with the little plaything which amused you so much this morning.'

She was so confused that she was unable to reply to me, and when I pressed my lips to her mouth she abandoned her hand to me and let me do with it as I liked. I made her bring my weapon up to an erect position along my belly and, opening a few buttons, introduced her hand within my trousers enabling her to have a better idea of the true nature of the organ of pleasure.

As she now made no objection to holding it in her hand and even began to caress it, I was in the act of raising my shirt to allow her to enjoy the pleasant feeling of the naked flesh, when we heard Eliza calling to her, saying that she was wanted and that Fanny must come and take her place at the piano. There was no alternative but to button up my trousers and gallop back to the drawing room, leaving her further enlightenment to be accomplished at a more convenient opportunity.

It was some days, however, before I could discover one that gave any promise of success.

There was to be an archery party given by a gentleman who resided at the distance of about twelve miles from us, and I fancied that in the course of the day I might find some opportunity of detaching Fanny from the rest of the company and accomplishing my object.

Owing to the presence of other visitors, none of the old ladies of the Abbey were able to go; but Mrs and Miss Vickars were to accompany the young people. Fanny was allowed to go with us in the Abbey carriage, which could be thrown open, and Mrs and Miss Vickars went in their own chaise; but I heard Mrs Vickars say to her daughter that she had better arrange to return at night in the Abbey carriage and send Fanny with her. This hint was not lost upon me, and failing all other means I devised a scheme founded upon it.

Despite all my efforts I was unable to make any progress with Fanny all day, beyond giving her a few slight caresses which only tended to inflame and increase my ardour, and I have no doubt they had pretty much the same effect upon her. She either did not or would not understand the hints I gave her to induce her to separate herself from her companions and give me the opportunity I so longed for, and without attracting observation, I was unable to press her.

There was to be a dance in the evening and we prevailed upon the old ladies to remain for it, so that it was quite dark when we started to return home. In the course of the evening I pressed Fanny to drink a few glasses of wine to prepare her for the scene I anticipated; but she would only take a single glass, until shortly before we set out, when she asked me to bring a glass of water. I said it was not good for her to drink cold water while she was overheated, but offered to get what I was drinking myself, a tumbler of soda water with a glass of champagne in it, which she agreed to take. I however reversed the prescription and brought her a tumbler of champagne with a glass of soda water. She drank off about half of it without discovering the deceit, and then laid it down, saying it was too strong. I said that anything she had tasted was too precious to be wasted and finished the tumbler.

In the course of the evening I took an opportunity of saying to Mrs Vickars, that as we should have to return in the dark, she might perhaps like to be accompanied by a gentleman, and that if she wished it, I would take the seat on the box beside the coachman. She said she would be very glad to have my escort; but that there was no occasion for my going outside as there was only to be herself and Fanny in the chaise, and there was plenty of room for me.

This was exactly what I wanted, and accordingly I most willingly agreed to her suggestion. Our carriage came first to the door, I handed Mrs Vickars in, then Fanny, and jumped in myself. It was one of those roomy old-fashioned chaises which could hold three people; but as the old lady was rather of an unusual size, a third seat, projecting forward, had been inserted for Fanny in the middle, which could be raised up or lowered down as required, and which consequently formed a sort of separation between the parties in the two corners.

Fanny had placed herself on this seat, but as it did not suit my purpose that she should remain there, I, without saying a word, removed her to the corner, and took her place. The night had become stormy and wet, and I enveloped Mrs V in a large cloak, ostensibly to protect her from the cold, but in reality to muffle her up and separate her as much as possible from us. Under the same pretext I threw a scarf over Fanny and myself, contriving at the same time to get our knees interlaced together, so as to have one of my legs between hers.

To keep up appearances, I began a conversation with the old lady, which I was convinced would not last long on her part. Under the cover of this, I soon got possession of Fanny's hand, and after some little toying, to divert her attention from my object, I placed it on my thigh, and again made her feel the stiff object which she had previously seen and felt. She resisted a little at first, but I persevered and, as curiosity, or perhaps desire, seemed in the end to prevail, I was convinced I might safely proceed further.

Having thus broken the ice, I removed her hand, and taking off her glove, pressed it to my lips, and threw one arm around her waist, so as to bring her close to me, while with the other hand I unbuttoned my trousers, and throwing them completely open, laid bare my organ of manhood with the adjacent part of my belly and thighs. Then suddenly bringing down her hand, I made her grasp the stiff naked pillar. This proceeding took her quite by surprise, and she allowed her hand to remain encircling the throbbing object for a few seconds, during which I felt a peculiar sort of tremor pass through her frame. But presently, recollecting herself, she attempted to withdraw her hand and remove herself from my embrace. She was, however, so shut up in the corner of the carriage that she was unable to get away from me and I managed to retain hold of her hand, and soon made it resume its position, closing her fingers round the symbol of manhood. Finding that she could not help herself, she ceased to struggle, and in a few minutes she not only made no attempt to withdraw her hand, but even allowed me to make it wander over all the adjacent parts, which I thought were likely to excite her curiosity and afford her pleasure to touch.

Having succeeded so far, I considered it advisable to make a diversion to distract her attention from the main object of which I wished to gain possession. I had ascertained that her dress, which had been changed to a low-breasted one for the dancing party, was fastened by buttons behind. I contrived to unloosen two of them, which made the part in front open and fall down, so as fully to disclose the two voluptuous globes of firm, springy flesh which adorned her bosom. My hand and lips took instant

79

possession of them and revelled in the through enjoyment of all their beauties. She moved about uneasily at first under this new attack, but when I slipped one of her nipples into my mouth, and began to suck it, she allowed her head to sink back and left me at liberty to pursue my amorous propensities as I thought fit.

I was perfectly certain now, from the convulsive manner in which her fingers occasionally closed around the staff of life, that her passions had become sufficiently excited and I thought I might venture on an attack in the proper quarter. Stooping down, I inserted my hand beneath her petticoat, and rapidly raised it up along her leg and thigh until it rested on the mount of pleasure. At the same time I advanced my knee between hers, so that it was impossible for her to close her legs, and bent myself over her so as to prevent her from deranging my position by her struggles. It required all my address to maintain my position and calm her first agitation. She struggled so violently at first, on finding her virgin territory thus rudely invaded, than I greatly feared she would disturb the old lady and excite her suspicions. I whispered softly to her to beware of this, adding that I would do nothing but what would give her pleasure.

The precautions I had taken prevented her from being able to offer any effectual resistance to me without making her grandmother aware of what was going on; and she probably felt that after having allowed me to go so far, she had lost the power of checking my further proceedings except at the risk of compromising herself. This, joined with the insidious effect which my voluptuous caresses must have by this time produced upon her senses, soon brought about the state of matters which I desired. Her struggles gradually became weaker, and I was at length left in full possession of the outworks.

As soon as I was satisfied of this, I felt that my object was gained, and I determined not to hurry on too rapidly to the conclusion, but to attempt to bring her by degrees to be as desirous for it as I was myself. I therefore allowed my hand to wander for some time over the soft expanse of her belly and thighs, playing with the silky tresses which surrounded the mount of pleasure and tickling and caressing the tender lips. I then gently separated them, and allowed a finger to insinuate itself a short way within the soft furrow, at the same time covering her mouth and bosom with repeated and burning kisses. When she first felt the intruding finger penetrating into the virgin sanctuary, which had never yet been invaded by the hand of another, she involuntarily drew back as if frightened and hurt.

Anxious to reassure her, I ceased to force it further in, and contented myself with moving it gently backwards and forwards between the lips. When she was somewhat reconciled to this, I sought out the little sensitive object – the titillation of which affords a girl so much pleasure. When I pressed it, she gave a start, but it was accompanied with such a peculiar pressure upon my own organ of pleasure that I felt convinced she was now sensible of the sympathetic feeling which exists between the two, and that she had already begun to experience the foretaste of the lascivious sensations I was desirous of rousing. I contined to press and tickle the little protruberance and occasionally to thrust my finger a little further into the crevice, until I felt her limbs become somewhat relaxed, and her thighs open wider mingled with some indescribable symptoms of the approach of the crisis of pleasure. I redoubled my titillations, now forcing my finger more boldly up and down the narrow entrance, until a few involuntary movements in response to my lascivious proceedings, and a long-drawn half-stifled sigh, announced the access of the voluptuous swoon. Her head sank on my shoulder, her fingers lost the grasp they had for some time firmly maintained upon my burning staff, and I felt a slight moisture oozing out and bedewing my finger as she paid the first tribute to Venus, which had been drawn from her by the hand of another.

When I was convinced the crisis was past, I withdrew my finger, and allowed her to remain quiet for a few minutes, during which I prepared both myself and her for the still more voluptuous encounter. I contemplated. She was now quite passive in my hands, and allowed me to raise up her petticoats, and fasten them around her waist, so as not to interfere with the delicious contact of our bodies which I now wished to effect. At the same time I allowed my trousers to fall to my knees, and tucked up my shirt under my waistcoat, so as to be prepared for the encounter.

The conversation between Mrs Vickars and me, which had been very languidly maintained on my part, had now entirely ceased; and the old lady was giving audible tokens that she was not in a condition to pay any attention to our proceedings. I was determined to take advantage of the opportunity to the utmost, and even if I should find myself unable to achieve the victory over the delicious maidenhead in prospect, I wished to make a beginning, by allowing the proper weapon to enter the premises in such a manner as to insure the certainty of his again being allowed to revisit them on any more favourable opportunity. I was, however, at a loss at first how to accomplish this. I was afraid to leave my seat and get upon her, for fear the old lady might suddenly awake and miss me from her side, and I was equally afraid of taking Fanny on my knee.

At length I determined on the following plan: I made her place herself on her left side, bringing her body so far forward that her hip rested on the edge of the cushion of the seat, thus presenting her bottom to me, which, as her clothes were turned up round her waist, was of course quite bare. I placed myself also on my left side, and brought my belly in delicious contact with her charming soft buttocks. The feeling that this produced was so exquisite that I was almost maddened; and it was with the greatest difficulty that, when I found my weapon nestling between the two delicious soft mounts of naked flesh, I could maintain sufficient command over myself to proceed with the moderation necessary to prevent discovery. I then raised up her right leg and inserted my own right leg between her thighs, at the same time drawing her to me, so as to bring the lower part of my belly as far forward between her legs as possible. Then shifting the position of my weapon from its resting place between her lovely buttocks, I lowered my body a little, till I could move forward the champion between her thighs, so that, on my raising myself up again, it reared its proud crest upwards along her belly, rubbing against the soft smooth flesh, almost up to her navel. I remained in this charming position for a few minutes, till she got over the alarm occasioned by the first contact of our naked bodies; and till I had quite satisfied myself that my position was such that I should have no difficulty in effecting the object I had in view.

When I thought she was sufficiently prepared, I lowered the point of the weapon till I brought it to nestle between the soft ringlets which adorned the mouth of the entrance to the grotto of pleasure. Then gently inserting my finger, I distended the lips as far as possible, and pressed the head of my champion forwards against the narrow slit with so much impetuosity that tight as it was, I felt the lips distend, and the point of the weapon penetrate within, until the head was wholly enclosed within the narrow precincts. I found, however, that I was proceeding too rapidly. Whether from the pain or the fright at this novel proceeding, Fanny uttered a cry which she seemed unable to suppress, and put down her hand, trying to remove the intruder from the place which he had so rashly invaded. I succeeded in preventing this and in maintaining my position; but I was sadly afraid she might have awakened the old lady, and I was obliged to remain quiet and not attempt to force myself further in, until I was quite satisfied from her quiet breathing that she still slumbered. I then ventured to whisper to Fanny for heaven's sake to remain quiet, that I would take every care not to hurt her, and that she would soon enjoy the most delicious pleasure.

I presume that the pain attendant on my first entrance had now somewhat abated, for without speaking she remained quiet and made no objection to my further progress. I tried to manage matters as tenderly as possible, proceeding to improve my position by slow degrees and merely pressing gently forward, without venturing to thrust with force. By this means I succeeded in getting nearly the half of the stiff stake fairly driven into her. But this slow mode of proceeding, though absolutely necessary in the circumstances, was maddening to me. My passions were wrought up to such a pitch by the lascivious manoeuvres I had been indulging in that I hardly knew what I was about; and every moment I was on the point of giving way to the fierce stimulus which urged me on, and endeavouring by one fierce thrust to plunge myself to the bottom and complete my enjoyment. I began also to feel that the struggle could not last much longer, for excited as I was I could no longer ward off the approach of the voluptuous crisis.

I was hesitating whether to run the risk of one final effort and burst through every obstacle at all hazards, or whether to rest contented with the imperfect enjoyment which my present situation could afford us both, when my hesitation was most disagreeably brought to an end by the carriage stopping and by the sound of the coachman's voice calling to someone in the road.

There was not a moment to be lost. I hastily withdrew my palpitating weapon from its delicious abode, pulled down Fanny's clothes, and without waiting to fasten my trousers, leaned forward to the side of the carriage away from the old lady and opened the window to ascertain the cause of the stoppage.

Fortunately I had taken the precaution to put on a light overcoat, which concealed the disordered state of my under garments. It appeared that the stoppage was merely occasioned by some carriers' carts which blocked up the way. They were speedily removed, and the carriage proceeded on. But as I had feared, the circumstance woke up the old lady. I satisfied her that there was no cause for alarm, and then remained silent, hoping that she would before long relapse into her slumber.

It was some time, however, before her nasal organs gave us the certainty that we might proceed with our amusement

84

in safety. As soon as we had got rid of the light from the lamps of the waggoners, I replaced Fanny in her previous position, without finding any opposition from her; but I did not venture to attempt the completion of my pleasing work, until I had the certainty that the old lady was not in a state to disturb us. In the meanwhile I played with her charms, and tickled and caressed the mount of pleasure; but I carefully refrained from again bringing on the fit of pleasure with her, as I wished to keep up her excitement and, if possible, make her participate with me in the delights of the closing scene.

At length I ventured to take up my old position, and did not find much impediment in getting my weapon within the entrance as far as I had reached previously. Having attained this point, however, I found the greatest difficulty in proceeding further. Every effort I made, evidently occasioned her the greatest pain; and though she strove to bear it patiently, I dreaded the consequences of her doing anything to rouse her grandmother's suspicions.

While I was still endeavouring by gentle means to accomplish my object, the excitement and the ardour of my pent-up passion proved too much for me. The paroxysm of delight seized upon me and forced me to shoot into her, with the greatest enjoyment on my part, but apparently to her great astonishment, a shower of the elixir of life, which, finding no passage in front, forced its way backwards through the tightly wedged-up channel, and poured out over her thighs. She remained quite motionless, evidently surprised at the unlooked for event which had occurred, and at my consequently sinking down upon her almost without the slightest appearance of animation. It was not long, however, before I recovered myself; and as my yet unsated passions held sufficient dominion over me to maintain the original stiffness of my throbbing weapon, I still kept him in his charming quarters, hoping that the lubrication I had now given to the channel might aid his progress and facilitate his further entry.

I was just flattering myself that I was about to accomplish

the complete success of my delightful task, when the carriage again stopped; and though we could hardly believe it, so rapidly had the time passed away, we found ourselves at the gate of the Abbey.

All hope of proceeding further was now at an end. We had merely time before we reached the house to wipe away the traces of my first exploit, which, as I reluctantly withdrew my still impetuous charger from his pleasant quarters, continued to pour down her thighs, and hastily to repair the disorder in our dress. As the carriage door was opened on the side of the old lady, I had time to give Fanny a sweet kiss, and to whisper in her ear that she must allow me to take the first opportunity of completing the lesson I had been giving her, for she had merely had a slight prelude of the pleasure it would afford her. My kiss was returned in a manner which gave me every reason to suppose she was as eager for the conclusion as I was.

It was now late, and all the party at the Abbey had retired to bed. We were ushered into the parlour, where we found wine and water and some refreshments prepared for us. Fanny pleaded fatigue, and retired to her own room almost immediately, afraid lest her agitation during the previous scene should have left any traces that might be discerned. But Mrs Vickars said that she would sit up until the carriage arrived. I told her I should remain with her, for it was no use going to bed to try to sleep as George would be sure to awaken me when he arrived.

We sat for half an hour, talking over the events of the day, until the old lady began to get alarmed at the non-arrival of the other party. I laughed at her fears at first, but as time wore on, I began to think some accident must have occurred, and at last I said that I would take my horse and ride back for a few miles to ascertain what had become of them. She urged me to take the carriage, but I said the horses had had a hard day's work, and that it was a pity to take them out again, unless it was absolutely necessary, but that I would tell the men not to go to bed and to be ready to start if they should be required. I went to the stable and had my horse saddled, and led it quietly out to the turf on the park and then set off at a good speed. I had only gone a mile or two from the park gate when I heard the sound of horses' feet approaching. I drew up, thinking that I would probably ascertain from the rider if any accident had occurred on the road.

He turned out to be a stable boy who had been sent from the place where we had spent the day to announce that our friends would not be able to reach home that night. It appeared that in passing the lodge, the coachman, who had probably been participating too freely in the hospitality of our friends, had run the carriage against a post, and although no one had suffered any injury, one of the wheels had been so much damaged that the carriage was unable to proceed. The ladies had been obliged to walk back to the house, and had got drenched in the rain, so that even if there had been another carriage at hand, which there was not, they could not have travelled in comfort. It had therefore been arranged that they should remain where they were for the night, and the messenger had been dispatched to prevent our being uneasy and to carry back some necessary change of dress, which would be required for them next morning.

I immediately turned my horse's head, and desiring the boy to follow me, returned to the Abbey. As I cantered up the avenue, my thoughts were naturally turned upon the scene which had occurred in the carriage, and the severe disappointment I had sustained in being unable to bring it to a satisfactory conclusion, and I began to consider in what manner I might still contrive to accomplish this.

After two or three schemes had passed through my mind, it occurred to me that I might not again find a combination of circumstances presenting so favourable an opportunity as was then afforded. Her aunt being absent, Fanny would pass the night alone, and George and the girls being also away, there was nothing to prevent me from spending it with her and completing the task I had only half accomplished. I made up my mind at least to make the attempt.

87

When I reached the house, the old lady's fears were soon allayed. The housekeeper, whom I found sitting with her, said she would get the things which were required for the young ladies without disturbing anyone in the house, and Mrs Vickars said she would go to Fanny's room to get what was wanted for her daughter.

I wished to make certain that she was not to remain for the night with Fanny, and I said I would get a clean shirt for George and bring a carpet bag to put all the things in. When Mrs Vickars returned I said I hoped Fanny had not been alarmed at her aunt's absence.

She replied, 'Oh, no'; that she had found her fast asleep, and not wishing to disturb her, had merely left a note on the table, mentioning what had occurred that she might find it when she awoke in the morning. This information was a great relief to me, for I had feared the possibility of some change of arrangements for the night, or that Fanny, finding she was to be left alone, might bolt the door and prevent me from gaining access to her.

I was not satisfied, however, until I had seen the old lady proceed to her own room, and even after the housekeeper had retired to her own domain, I watched at the door till I heard the old lady flop into bed and saw that the candle was extinguished.

Considering everything now quite safe, I hastened to my apartment, and stripped off every article of dress, putting on merely a pair of slippers and a dressing gown. Thus equipped, I cautiously made my way to Fanny's room, and softly opened the door, closing it again, and turning the key in the lock. The weather, by this time, had cleared up, and the moon was shining brightly into the room through the upper part of the window, the shutters of which had been left open. The first bed I came to was vacant, but the other presented a most delicious sight.

My movements had been so quiet that Fanny had not been disturbed, and was still fast asleep. But from her situation, it would appear that her slumber had not altogether been unbroken. She lay on her back, with one

88

arm raised up and resting on her head. The bed clothes had been pushed down, nearly as far as her waist, disclosing the form of her bosom, and her chemise being loosely fastened hung down at one side, and gave me a perfect view of one of her lovely bubbies, with its ivory expanse tipped with the purple nipple.

I sat down on the bed beside her, and gazed for a while with delight on her budding charms. But it was impossible long to continue myself merely to their view, delicious as it was. Bending my head down, I imprinted burning kisses on her lovely mouth and exquisite breasts.

This soon roused her from her slumber, but at first she was unconscious of my presence. Moving herself uneasily, but without opening her eyes, she said, 'Is that you, Aunt?'

My first idea had been to jump into bed beside her, and, before she could prevent me, get possession of her person so far as to secure the object I had in view, but I was afraid that, if suddenly awakened in this manner, she might, before recognizing me, call out for assistance, and thus alarm the house. Besides, after what had passed I did not now expect any serious opposition to bring her gradually round to participate with me in all the delight I anticipated, than to attempt to snatch it from her unawares. I therefore repeated my kiss, and whispered gently, 'No, dearest, it is not your aunt, but it is one who loves you a great deal better.'

She started at the sound of my voice, and opened her eyes. At first she seemed scarcely to know who it was, but as soon as she recognised me, she raised herself up, and sitting erect, exclaimed, 'Frank! Is it you? What is the matter? What has brought you here? Good heavens! Something dreadful must have happened! Where is my aunt?' I attempted to soothe her, telling her there was nothing to fear, and explaining the accident that had occurred to the carriage.

She would not believe for some time that I was telling her all the truth, and insisted upon reading the note, which I said her grandmother had left, asking me to light a candle that she might be able to do so.

The bed curtains were drawn back at the head of the bed, and close to it stood a large cheval glass with two wax candles on each side, I saw the good use I might put this to, and lighting one of the candles I gave the note to her to read.

While she did so, I hastily lighted the other candle, and then standing upright by the bedside, I allowed my dressing gown, my only covering, to open out fully in front, and drew it back, so as to expose the whole of the forepart of my naked person.

When Fanny had finished the purusal of the note, she raised up her eyes and the first thing they rested upon was my throbbing priapus, which the sight of her charms had roused up to a brilliant state of erection.

As soon as she caught a glimpse of it, her face and neck became suffused with crimson, and she raised her hands to cover her eyes, exclaiming, 'Oh, Frank! Frank! How could you come here in such a state?'

'You should rather say, my own darling,' was my reply, 'how could I help coming here after what has taken place tonight, and when I found there was such a favourable opportunity of happily completing the work we were so pleasantly engaged in, and which we were obliged to leave unfinished. You cannot yet imagine half the pleasure it will give us to bring it to a successful conclusion.'

It was a considerable time before I was able to soothe her, and to satisfy her that there was no risk to be apprehended from my remaining with her, for a part, at least, of the night. But I succeeded at length in convincing her that the house was closed for the night, and everyone was gone to bed. I told her besides that even in case anyone should come to her door, and wish to get admittance, I could easily escape by the window, and reach my own rooms without discovery.

Even after I had relieved her anxiety on this point, I had some difficulty in persuading her to let me get into bed with her. At length this was conceded on the condition that I was not to take off my dressing gown, and was only to get between the blankets, and not to get under the sheets, or meddle with anything below her bosom, which, with her mouth, was to be given up to my caresses.

It may easily be supposed that this being conceded the conditions were not long observed, or even insisted upon. My dressing gown was soon slipped off. During the caresses which I claimed the right to bestow as being within the terms of our agreement, it was very easy for me to remove the coverings which intervened between us, and without much resistance I soon brought our two naked bodies into close contact with each other.

Having now no fear of interruption, I was in no hurry to urge on the completion of my pleasing work. I wished rather by a short delay, and by making use of all the little charming excitements which are so pleasing both to give and to receive, to rouse up her passions to an equal pitch with my own, and to make her as eager as myself for the enjoyment of the coming bliss. I therefore continued for some time the prelude, by the most amorous touches and titillations which I could devise, extending them to every part of her naked body, making her in return perform the same pleasing operations on the corresponding parts of my own person.

This at first she hesitated to do, but she very soon got warmed and excited, and without any hesitation began to put into practice every wanton trick I suggested. I saw that my object was fully attained, and that she was quite ready to co-operate with me in the crowning work. I whispered to her that I was afraid she must still have to submit to a little further pain before we could be perfectly happy, but that I would do all in my power to prevent her suffering and that she would soon be amply rewarded for what she must undergo by the supreme bliss it would enable us to attain.

I then placed her in a proper position to enable me to complete the enterprise. As I was quite aware that I had not yet effected a thorough penetration, and was afraid that there might be some sanguinary tokens of my victory, I arranged her on her back with my dressing gown underneath her, to prevent any stains reaching the sheets. Then separating her legs, and getting on my knees between them, I bent myself forward until I brought the point of the weapon to the mouth of the lovely sheath, into which I wished to plunge it.

When she saw me kneeling before her, with the palpitating weapon fully extended and standing out stiffly before me, she raised on hand to her eyes, as if ashamed to look it fairly in the face. But I seized upon the other hand and made her, not unwillingly, take hold of the extended lance, and maintain it in the proper position, while with my own fingers on each side I gently distended the lips of the cavity, so as to open up an entrance for it. Bending still further forward and leaning down upon her, I pressed the burning weapon into the fiery furnace of love, and as soon as I felt that the point had fairly gained admittance within the gates, I thrust onwards with fierce heaves of my buttocks. But the fortress was not to be gained possession of so easily. I penetrated without much difficulty as far as I had previously reached, but there I was again arrested by an obstacle that seemed almost invincible, without using a degree of force which I was anxious, if possible, to avoid. I soon found, however, that there was no alternative. The closely confined manner in which the point and the upper portion of love's instrument was pent up within the narrow cavity produced such an intense irritation upon its sensitive surface that it drove me almost frantic and, combined with the excitement of my senses occasioned by the lascivious pranks we had been previously indulging in, gave me ample warning that it would be impossible long to refrain from pouring forth the blissful shower.

It would have been too bad to have been condemned a second time to waste all its fragrance on the unplucked flower, and I was determined to spare no endeavours to avoid so dire a calamity. Relaxing my efforts, therefore, for a few moments, I explained to Fanny the necessity for making a vigorous attack, and begged of her to endure it as well as she could, and to try to assist me as far as possible, assuring her that the pain would only be momentary, and would lead to exquisite bliss.

She was now almost as much excited and as eager for the fray as I was, and she readily promised to do her utmost to assist my efforts. Getting my arms round her waist, and making her cross her legs over my buttocks, so as to clasp me round the back, I withdrew the stiff member as far as I could without making it issue from its charming abode, and then with a steady, well-sustained, vigorous thrust, I sent it forward as forcibly as was within my power. I felt at once that I was accomplishing the wished for object. Everything gave way before the energetic manner in which I drove the sturdy champion forward, and I felt him every instant getting engulfed further and further within the narrow channel. This was confirmed by the delicious pressures of the lips which I felt closing round the upper part of the column in the most charming manner possible.

But if all this was delightful to me, it was far otherwise with poor Fanny. She evidently strove hard to keep her word and render me every assistance, but when I first burst through the opposing barrier, the fast hold she had hitherto maintained of me suddenly relaxed, and she uttered a piercing cry of pain. As I continued to force my way in, the pain seemed to increase, and she besought me, in piteous accents, to have compassion upon her and to desist. But I was now far too highly wrought up to be able to comply with her request, even if I had been disposed to do so, which I certainly was not for I was perfectly convinced that it would be the kindest thing I could do, to put an end to her sufferings forever by at once effecting a complete penetration.

There was no time to explain all this to her, so at the risk of appearing cruel, I persevered without any relaxation in my victorious career. Two or three more thrusts sufficed to lodge me within her to the very hilt, and I felt my belly come into delicious contact with her warm flesh, accompanied with the charming tickling sensation of her hair rubbing against me and mingling with mine.

Doubly animated by this exquisite contact, my frantic thrusts were renewed without any regard to poor Fanny's sufferings. But the feelings I endured were too delightful to be of long continuance; the pent-up tide within me could no longer be prevented from bursting forth, and with the most exquisite sensation of gratification and delight, it issued from me and found its way into her inmost cavities. Gasping and breathless with voluptuous joy, I sank down upon her bosom, no longer able even to imprint the amorous kisses on her lovely face with which I had been endeavouring to stifle her tender complaints.

After a few minutes spent in luxuriating in the blissful annihilation which follows complete fruition, I began to recover my senses a little. I was conscious that, during this period, Fanny had ceased to struggle, and was now lying motionless beneath me. I judged from this that the pain she had been suffering had by this time ceased, and I was anxious, as soon as possible, to make her participate in the delicious pleasure she had afforded me, but of which I was afraid she had as yet hardly had a taste.

The dart of love, though somewhat relaxed and diminished in size from the effects of the charming emission, still retained its position within her delightful grotto with sufficient vigour to assure me that in a short time it would be able to renew its career in the lists of love. I therefore determined to allow it to remain where it was, and thus avoid the difficulty and pain of effecting a new entrance.

Retaining my position upon her, I did all I could to soothe and calm poor Fanny. She was very much agitated, and had been sadly frightened by the impetuosity with which I had rushed on in my triumphant career without regard to the suffering she was enduring. At first she begged and prayed of me to get up, fearing that any renewal of the fierce transports I had indulged in would cause repetition of her agony.

To this, however, I would not agree, assuring her that she had no occasion to be alarmed, and that she had nothing to look forward to but transports of pleasure equal to those I had enjoyed. I soon convinced her of this, by two or three gentle thrusts of the weapon which had caused her so much discomfort, but which now, on the contrary, occasioned the most delightful sensations.

The passage having been fairly opened up and well lubricated by my first discharge, and the unruly member not being quite so fiercely distended as previously, it slipped up and down within her with the greatest of ease. Of course, at first I thrust with great caution, but I soon brought her to acknowledge that the pleasing friction it occasioned to her, so far from being disagreeable, afforded her the greatest delight; and even when our voluptuous movements produced their natural effect and stiffened and hardened the champion of love till it regained its full size and consistency, and again filled up the burning cavity till it was completely gorged and almost ready to burst, its presence within her and the fiercer and more rapid thrusts which I now allowed it to make, so far from being painful, evidently gave her intense delight. Her eyes now sparkled, and her cheeks blazed with voluptuous fires. She clasped her arms round me and drew me fondly to her bosom, while her lips returned the burning kisses which I imprinted upon her lovely mouth. Presently, no longer able to restrain herself, and losing every idea of modesty or bashfulness under the strong excitement produced by the voluptuous titillation which my inflamed organ of manhood exerted over her most sensitive parts, she twisted her legs around mine, she drew her thighs together, and contracted them closely to meet and increase the effect of every lascivious shove I gave her; she heaved her buttocks up and down in charming concert with my motions, so as to insure the most voluptuous and delicious effect from the alternate withdrawal and replacement of the weapon of love, which she took good care not to allow to escape entirely from its delightful prison. Finding her thus charmingly excited and enjoying herself to the utmost, I did all in my power to add to her bliss.

Being now a little calmer than I had been during the first

fierce onslaught of her virgin charms, I was able at first to control my own movements and to direct them in such a manner as I thought would afford her the greatest enjoyment – quite satisfied that in doing so, I was only paving the way to still greater bliss for myself. I therefore watched her carefully and moderated or increased my efforts as I fancied would be most agreeable to her, until I saw from her excited gestures that the final crisis was fast approaching with her. Desirous to participate in the bliss, I then gave full vent to my own maddening passions. I heaved and thrust with impetuous fury; I strained her in my arms; and at every thrust, given with more and more force and velocity, I strove to drive myself further and further within her delicious recess.

She responded to every effort I made; her legs clasped me tighter, her bottom heaved up and down with greater velocity and stronger impetus, and the delicious contraction of the lips of her warm moist grotto closed round my excited weapon with still greater and more charming constriction. She sobbed, she panted, her bosom heaved up and down, and she clung to me as if she would incorporate her every existence with mine. Her transports were quite sufficient, without any exertion on my part, to have produced the most delicious effect upon me, and I soon felt that, notwithstanding my previous discharge, I was quite ready to co-operate with her and to enjoy in unison the impending blissful sensation of the final crisis, I had not long to wait. A few upward heaves, more rapid and impetuous than ever – one last straining of her body to mine – and then the sudden relaxation of her tight grasp, accompanied with a heavy long-drawn sigh of pleasure, announced her participation for the first time in the joys of amorous coition. I was quite ready to join her – two or three active thrusts completed my bliss, and almost before her nectar had begun to flow, my voluptuous effusion was poured into her to mingle with her tide of rapture.

I raised my head to gaze on her lovely countenance, and to watch the gradations of pleasure as they flitted across her beautiful features, while with a few gentle motions of the champion, who had occasioned us so much delight, I spun out and completed the intoxicating bliss, till at length her eyes closed, the colour forsook her cheeks, and unconscious of what was passing around her, she sank into the blissful intoxication of completed desire.

After revelling for a few delightful minutes in the thorough enjoyment of my now perfectly completed victory, I withdrew my valiant champion reeking with the bloody tokens of success, and took up my position, with my head on the pillow beside her, before she had recovered the full possession of her senses.

I was in no hurry to rouse her from the trance of rapture. Although by no means disposed to allow the opportunity to escape me without profiting further by the conquest I had obtained, I felt that after the exertion I had made, I would be all the better for a little repose before attempting fresh exploits. I therefore lay quietly by her side for some time, hardly speaking and merely occasionally pressing her to my bosom and tasting the sweets of her lips and her bosom.

But when she had thoroughly recovered from the effects of her first enjoyment, I found that Fanny was now quite alive to the bliss to be derived from our pleasing conjunction; and that there would be no difficulty on her part at least to an immediate renewal of the amorous struggle. She reciprocated the fond caresses I lavished upon her, and even indulged herself in bestowing fresh ones upon me. I soon found that her curiosity was excited by the difference she found between my person and her own, and as I was quite disposed to gratify such a natural feeling, her hands were presently wandering over those parts of my body with which she was least familiar, but which recent events had taught her were the most attractive. I could perceive her surprise, and I thought her disappointment, when, without any assistance on my part, they reached the spot where the emblem of virility is situated, and when she found in her grasp, instead of the hard, stiffly-distended object which had penetrated her, causing first so much pain and then so much pleasure by its forcible entrance, a soft, limp mass of flesh which dangled between her fingers, and which she could twist around them in every direction.

I laughed at her surprise, and told her she must not always expect to find the little gentleman in the rampant condition in which she had hitherto seen him; that his present condition was his natural one, and that it was only the power of her charms that could rouse him up to action in his fierce excited state. She was soon able to judge for herself of the truth of my statement, for her wanton caresses were already beginning to produce their usual effect upon the little hero, who speedily erected and uncovered his rosy head, and extended himself at full length, swelling out till the ivory pillar quite filled up her grasp.

She was evidently not more surprised than gratified by this sudden resuscitation, and continued to tickle and play with it till I felt that it was not only in a suitable condition to renew the assault, but even that, if much longer delay, there was a danger of his yielding up his forces under her insidious blandishments before he was fairly ensconced in the citadel. I therefore told her that I could stand her wanton toying no longer, and that she must allow the little plaything again to take possession of the charming abode it had so recently entered, and there again offer up its adoration to her charms.

She readily agreed, though she expressed some fear lest its entrance should again cause a renewal of her sufferings. I told her there was not much fear of this, and that beyond a slight smart at the first penetration, she would in all probability find nothing but pleasure in the renewed encounter.

However, when I applied my hand to the charming spot for the purpose of separating the lips and preparing for the entrance, I found that the sanguine tide which had issued from her on my first withdrawal had now become encrusted on the curly moss which surrounded the entrance. I felt that it was quite necessary that all such traces of the conflict should be removed, and I thought that it would be more agreeable to us both that this should be done before we renewed the game of pleasure.

Turning down the bed-clothes, I proceeded to examine the spot more minutely and was somewhat shocked to find the traces of the ravages I had committed. She was a good deal frightened on seeing her thighs and the lower part of her belly covered with the crimson effusion, but I soon reassured her by explaining how it was occasioned; and the introduction of my finger within the orifice, where it could now penetrate with ease, convinced her that she had not much to fear from again admitting the somewhat larger plaything, which now throbbed under her grasp.

I was pleased to find that the precautions I had taken had prevented any marks which could induce suspicion. All that was necessary was to remove the bloody traces from our persons. This, I thought, would be best affected by means of the bidet. I accordingly made her get up and seat herself upon it. She was at first ashamed and reluctant to expose her naked person so completely to my gaze, for the candles I had lighted, reflected from the mirror, threw a brilliant light over all her secret charms; but my praises of their beauty, joined to the warm caresses I indulged in, at length reconciled her to the novel situation and she soon began to return my caresses.

Taking a sponge, I quickly removed all traces of the fierce combat, but as she seemed to be gratified by the application of the cool refreshing liquid to her heated spring of pleasure, I continued for some time to bathe the entrance to the charming grotto. She had now gained courage to take a fair survey of the wicked monster, as she called it, which had so cruelly ravaged her secret charms, and which now held up its crested head in a haughty manner, as if threatening to commit new devastations in the pleasant country he had so lately passed through. He bore, however, evident tokens of the bloody fray, and she laughingly said that I stood as much in need of the application of the purifying water as she did. I told her that as I had already performed the cleansing operation upon her, it was her turn now to do so upon me, and giving her the sponge, I sat down upon the bidet facing her, and throwing my arms round her neck, began to caress her charming bubbies.

She commenced to apply the sponge to remove the traces of the combat from my person, and was greatly amused to find the almost instantaneous effect which the sudden application of the cold water had upon the rampant object, which stood upright between my legs. In a few instants its head was lowered, and presently it dangled down, dropping its crest, and hanging over the pendulant globules, till it reached the water in the bidet.

After enjoying her amusement for a while, I told her that it was only her fair hand that could repair the mischief she had occasioned, and that she must take it between her fingers and coax it to hold up its head again. This she willingly did, and her potent charms soon effected a complete resurrection.

She had expressed so much gratification at the effect which the cooling liquid had produced in allaying the irritation of the entrance to her grotto that I proposed to her to try whether we could not manage to pump up some of the soothing fluid within its recesses. She laughed, and asked how this could be done.

I told her I would show her. I made her stand up, and seating myself properly on the bidet I made her get astride upon me, then holding the erected weapon in the proper direction I caused her to sink down upon me until it had fairly penetrated the lovely chink which was thus presented to it. When I felt that it was fully entered, I placed my hands on her buttocks on each side, and leant back so as to enable her to seat herself across the upper part of my thighs, with my weapon still penetrating her. I then told her to move herself gently up and down upon the stiff stake which impaled her, but to take care not to rise so high as to allow it to escape from its confinement.

When I had just made it enter, she winced a little, but I believe it was more from fear than from any actual pain; but as soon as it had reached its fullest extent within her, she seemed relieved from all apprehension and willingly commenced the work of pleasure. Indeed she was so earnest in it and moved up and down so rapidly that I was obliged, in order to carry out my design, to ask her to moderate her transports. Filling the sponge with water, I introduced it between our bellies, and every time she rose up leaving my member exposed I squeezed the sponge so as to cover it with water, and then made her again sink down upon it and engulf it.

It is true that the tight-fitting nature of the sheath which thus received it, prevented much of the water from being forced up into the inner receptacle – still the pleasing coolness which was produced by the constant bathing of the heated member and which was thus in some degree transferred to her burning interior was by her account most agreeable, and certainly I found the effect upon myself equally so. The intermittent action of the hot receptacle into which it was alternately plunged prevented any bad effects from the cold application, and my unruly member, instead of being weakened by it, was rather invigorated and urged on to fresh and more strenuous action. We continued this pleasing amusement for some time till we both got too much excited and too eager for the completion of our final enjoyment to be able to endure the delay between each thrust which this proceeding occasioned.

My buttocks heaved up, and she sank down so rapidly upon the pleasure giving stake, that I was forced to abandon my occupation. At length roused to a pitch of fury, I made her throw her arms around my neck, and placing my hands under her lovely bottom I rose up carrying her along with me without dislodging my enchanted weapon from its charming abode, and making her bottom rest on the edge of the bed and twisting her legs around my loins, I thrust and drove my vigorous engine into her with the greatest energy and pleasure. She had been as much excited as I had been by our amorous play, and she now responded most willingly and satisfactorily to my lascivious pushes. A few moments of the most exquisite enjoyment followed, which every succeeding thrust brought to a higher pitch of perfection, until our senses, being taxed to the utmost degree of voluptuous pleasure which it is possible to endure, gave way and, pouring out our souls in a delicious mutual effusion, we sank down on the bed in the most extreme delight.

After this charming exploit, we both felt the necessity for some little repose, and ere long we were fast locked in slumber in each other's arms. The rays of the morning sun roused me and warned me of the necessity for taking my departure before any of the servants should get up and observe me returning to my own room.

Fanny was still fast asleep, but the view I had of her naked charms which were exposed half uncovered by the bed-clothes, rendered it absolutely impossible for me to leave her without again offering up my homage to them, and the splendid condition in which my little champion, invigorated by a few hours repose, reared up his proud crest along her belly, as she lay clasped in my arms, convinced me that he was quite prepared to do his duty. There was no time to be lost. Without waking Fanny, I lowered the head of the throbbing weapon to the spot of pleasure, and insinuated it within it as gently as possible. I met with no resistance. She made a few uneasy movements as I slowly inserted the weapon; but, overcome with the fatigues and emotion of the previous night she still slept on. I would fain have remained in my delicious quarters, and spun out my pleasure to the utmost; but time pressed, and I was forced to make the most of it. My motions became more and more excited and energetic.

At length, roused by the efforts of the pleasure-stirring instrument within her, Fanny opened her eyes, and for a moment gazed with wonder upon me.

A fond kiss and a home thrust soon brought her to herself. Without a word the kiss was returned and the thrust responded to with hearty good will. A delicious contest ensued, each striving who would first reach the goal of pleasure; and certainly, if her raptures on attaining it equalled mine, she had nothing to complain of.

We had hardly concluded the pleasing enjoyment, when a noise we heard in the house rendered it absolutely necessary I should leave her, and I fortunately reached my own apartment without being observed.

The Power of Mesmerism

*A highly erotic narrative of
voluptuous facts and fancies*

Brackley Hall was a fine old place in the lovely country of Devon and had been in the possession of the Etheridges for centuries.

The park was beautifully wooded, and stretched down on one side to the coast, commanding in all directions the most enchanting views.

Mr Etheridge was a man of some forty years of age, of singularly handsome appearance, and bore evident traces of the Italian blood which flowed in his veins. He had the appearance of a man having strong amorous passions, but his manners were as gentle as those of a woman, and he was universally popular throughout the whole country.

His wife was a woman of unusual beauty. Descended from an old Spanish family, she had married when but sixteen years of age; Mr Etheridge having met her at the house of some friends, and as they mutually fell in love with each other, their united entreaties overcame the objection raised on account of her youth, and in fact the warm blood that flowed in her veins had ripened her beauty to an extent almost unusual in those of more phlegmatic races.

She was now in her thirty-fifth year, and in the full zenith of her charms. An exquisitely shaped head graced a neck and shoulders white as alabaster, large liquid eyes, and long drooping lashes, a nose of perfect form, and two ruby pouting lips that seemed made to be kissed.

Her form was magnificent, of commanding height, widely spreading hips, and a bosom of massive proportions, the firmness of which rendered stays entirely unnecessary; a fact that was evident on watching the rise and fall of those two lovely globes, their form being perfectly defined even to

107

the nipples, beneath her well-fitting dress.

Her glance was electric, and it was impossible to meet her look unmoved, she exhaled an atmosphere of voluptuousness of the most maddening force.

Her daughter Ethel, who had left school in Paris but a few months, was the very counterpart of her lovely mother in her leading features. She had just completed her seventeenth year, and was of tall, graceful stature, with a perfect figure. The smallness of her waist contrasted perfectly with the ravishing fullness of bosom and wideness of hips. She had the liquid eyes of her mother, but they were suffused with a humidity that was perfectly maddening, and the expression of every feature of her lovely face and lascivious abandon that would have tempted an anchorite.

On a bright summer afternoon, in the year 18 – , father, mother, and daughter were waiting at the railway station, anxiously expecting the arrival of the remaining member of the family. Frank, who, a year older than Ethel, had been finishing his education in Germany, and was now returning to take up his residence at Brackley.

At last the train arrived, and they hardly recognised the handsome, tall, and fine-looking young fellow who leaped out to greet them.

A few hours after reaching the house the parents noted a peculiar change that had taken place in their son. A dreamy languor seemed to have taken possession of him, in place of the exuberant flow of animal spirits that characterized him as a boy. He had a strange habit of looking as though he were endeavouring to read the very thoughts of those with whom he came in contact.

Mrs Etheridge noticed this particularly, but thinking he was fatigued by his long journey, made no remark. But the most remarkable effect was produced on Ethel; her brother seemed utterly unable to remove his eyes from her. Her singular beauty, and the nameless charm that pervaded her, seemed to have an irresistible attraction for him. Every time that his eyes rested on her she trembled violently, and seemed labouring under some mysterious and powerful influence. Her lovely breasts heaved, and the humidity of her eyes increased, and she still seemed unusually excited after her brother had left the room in order to dress for dinner.

Some friends had been invited to dine, and Frank found himself placed between his mother and sister. He glanced alternatively at the two lovely bosoms, well exposed by the low dresses each of them wore; and hs face flushed, and he seemed for the moment about to faint, but almost immediately recovering himself, he proceeded with his dinner and joined in the conversation.

In the course of the meal he ventured again to glance at his sister, and as she was leaning forward he saw the lovely valley between those hills of snow.

He accidently pressed his knee against hers, she immediately looked at him fondly, and her breasts rose and fell tumultuously as she mechanically pressed closer to him.

Nothing further happened on this occasion, but they had a most charming evening in the drawing room, and Ethel and Frank seemed to have formed a more than usually close friendship. They had not seen each other for four years, and their reunion seemed a source of the greatest delight to both of them. Mrs Etheridge also inspired her son with the most intense affection.

Before retiring for the night Frank proposed an early walk on the grounds, as he was anxious to renew his acquaintance with all the spots so attractive to him when a boy, and Ethel joyously assented. Six o'clock was agreed to, which would leave them two good hours until breakfast time.

When Ethel retired to rest she was in a state of wild excitement and could not banish her darling brother's image from her thoughts.

At length she fell into a troubled sleep, and after tossing wildly about, awoke suddenly and found that she was spending, her nightdress and chemise were saturated, and her lovely cunt was throbbing with the ecstacy. She was no stranger to this sensation (as the reader will subsequently learn) as she habitually produced the result with her fingers;

but this emission seemed more madly exciting than any she had ever felt before, and was produced without the usual means. At length she fell asleep again, but dreamt continually of her brother.

He, for his part, was mentally exercising a power he had acquired in Germany (the peculiar circumstances of the manner in which he gained this knowledge will be duly explained later on), and this was sufficient to account for his sister's condition.

Punctually at six o'clock on the following morning, brother and sister met in the hall. She threw herself into his arms and embraced him with great affection. 'You darling brother,' said she, 'how glad I am to have you back with us; it seems like a new world to me.'

'My dearest sister,' replied he, 'it is I who am the happy one, I cannot express to you the delight and happiness I feel in your society, after so long an absence.'

After embracing again they started on their ramble; Ethel pointed out all her pet flowers and every spot that she liked, until they found themselves, at length, in a charming little grove overhanging the beach.

'Frank, darling,' said she, 'I have a headache; shall we sit down here and rest a short time until it goes away?'

'Certainly, my darling, and I think I can relieve that headache by a simple expedient I learned in Germany.'

He then sat down opposite to her, and taking her two thumbs held them in the palm of his left hand, while with the right he made passes from her head to her feet, at the same time gazing into her eyes with a literally devouring look.

As he proceeded the humidity in her lovely eyes increased until the eyelids at last closed, and her head sank on her bosom.

After continuing the passes for a short time longer, her brother, still keeping his eyes fixed on her, gradually allowed her hands to slip away from his, and fall on her lap. He appeared intensely excited, his nostrils were dilated, he breathed hard, and his eyes seemed to burn in their sockets.

He gently laid Ethel down on her back, and after waiting to satisfy himself that she was in a fast mesmeric sleep, he placed one throbbing hand on her hip, and gradually raising it till he found the lovely prominence of one charming bosom, then his other hand sought its companion, and he pressed those heaving hills of snow which he felt perfectly under her thin muslin dress. He next knelt down by her side, and brought her breasts fully to view; they were indeed lovely, the two little pink nipples were stiffly erected, and seemed wooing to be kissed. She wore no stays, and his hand wandered over her lovely velvety skin down to her enchanting belly. Then rising, he leant forwards and gradually raised her dress in front.

First, her lovely ankles were seen, then her swelling calves, beautifully shaped knees, and glorious thighs. Frank felt faint and sick, and was compelled to desist from further exploration till he had somewhat recovered.

In a few moments he gently separated those divine thighs, and his eyes were riveted on his sister's darling little cunt, which now lay fully exposed to view. Two lovely coral lips, which were slight parted, moist and throbbing, first met his gaze. He separated them yet further with his finger and saw the exquisite clitoris perfectly visible. Utterly unable to resist the temptation, he glued his lips to the lovely spot, and titillated the clitoris with his tongue. Almost immediately she began to writhe and twist about, and he felt her balmy emission flow into his mouth as she spent with low moans. He then desisted, and releasing his bursting prick commenced slowly to frig himself, while gazing on the exquisite beauties exhibited to his view. With spasmodic jerks the semen flew from him while he moaned with pleasure.

Now fearing discovery, he carefully wiped his sister's cunt with his handkerchief, which he madly kissed afterwards, and adjusted her dress, removed all traces of his own spending, and proceeded to awaken his sister. Placing her in a sitting position against a tree, he recommenced his passes, this time in a contrary direction, and she soon after

111

opened her eyes.

After looking at him vaguely for a moment, she flung her arms round his neck, and kissed him. 'Oh,' she said, 'I have been asleep, and had such a delicious dream.'

'Has your headache gone?' said he.

'Oh,' she replied, 'I did have a headache, but not a symptom of it remains.'

She was evidently utterly unconscious of all that had taken place, and her brother suggested they should resume their walk.

At breakfast Mrs Etheridge said, 'You have had a walk betimes this morning, my children, and you are both looking quite rosy.'

So they were, but she little knew the cause.

After breakfast Mr Etheridge addressed himself to his son. 'Your mamma and myself are obliged to go to Lynton this afternoon on family business, and I fear we shall not be able to return until late, but I have no doubt you will be able to amuse yourself; Ethel will, I am sure, do her best to keep you from getting dull on your first arrival at home, after so long an absence.'

When they had started, Frank accompanied Ethel into her sitting room, and begged her to sing and play for him, in order that he might hear what progress she had made.

She at once complied with his request, and he sat by her side watching with glaring eyes the rise and fall of her lovely bosom as she sang him a charming little song, full of simple natural tenderness. He was, in fact, lusting madly for his own sister, and why not?

In the earliest history of our own race incest was no sin; why should we now consider it as such? On the other hand what can be more intensely exciting than the knowledge that one is indulging every feeling of lasciviousness conjointly with one united so nearly by ties of blood and kindred.

When she had finished he burned to enjoy her, but dared not, and with an effort he left the room, saying that he had some letters to write.

He went to his bedroom, but on his way thither he saw the adjoining door open and recognized a dress his sister had worn on the previous evening hanging against the wall. Her bed was still unmade, her nightdress was lying on it, and by the side of the bed a pair of drawers that she left there on changing her underlinen. He rushed to the bed, kissed the nightdress, and literally glued his lips to that portion of her drawers which had covered her darling little cunt. He was so excited that he could scarcely forbear from spending on the spot. Hearing approaching footsteps he immediately made his way to his own room, and bolting the door, he tore off his trousers. Doubling up the pillow, he inserted his prick between the folds, and straining it tightly between his thighs, threw himself forward on the bed, and thinking of his darling sister, with a few heaves backwards and forwards, spent deliciously. He then lay down and pondered over the best means of attaining his desires, for he resolved that he would enjoy his sister in every conceivable manner, let the consequences be what they might.

His meditations were interrupted by the luncheon bell. He descended to the dining room, and the sight of his sister aroused his desires with redoubled force; he devoured her with his eyes, and she again exhibited the same restless and uncomfortable symptoms that possessed her in the morning; her colour rose, her bosom rose and fell tumultuously, she squeezed her thighs together, sighed deeply, and seemed altogether unlike herself.

Seeing this he averted his gaze, and commenced talking on indifferent subjects. When the servants had left the room, he suggested another stroll on the grounds, as it was such a lovely afternoon. She consented with delight, and they set forth.

After rambling some distance from the house, she said, 'Frank, my darling, there is such a lovely summer house in this thicket where I often come and read, shall we go in and rest?'

Frank was delighted at the idea. It was a charming little retreat, completely hidden by trees, and furnished most luxuriously – a velvet couch, an easy chair, and a lounge occupying the whole of one side invited to repose.

They sat down, and Frank's arm wound round his sister's enticing waist, and he could not resist kissing those lovely pouting lips. She trembled like an aspen, and as he gazed into her moist and humid eyes, the strange symptoms reappeared.

Frank could no longer resist, but holding her thumbs he commenced the magnetic passes, and she speedily fell into his arms, apparently in a deep slumber. He now sought to see if he was entirely successful in his attempt to produce the effect he desired, and therefore taking her in his arms and laying her on the couch, he said. 'Ethel, do you know where you are?'

'With my darling brother,' she replied.

'Do you love him?'

'Madly,' was the reply.

'What would you like to do to prove that love?'

'Anything he desires.'

'Stand up.'

She did so.

'Unfasten your dress; take it off.'

She complied immediately.

'Loosen your petticoats and take them off: now your slippers and your stockings.'

The dear girl did exactly as requested, still in the same dreamy, languid manner. She now stood in her chemise and drawers only, and Frank felt as if he would faint. This splendid girl standing before him; lovely ankles, calves, and bare feet and those enchanting breasts peeping over her embroidered chemise, constituted a most voluptuous sight.

'Now, my darling,' said he, 'remove your drawers.'

She did so, and he snatched them up and covered them with kisses.

'Now the chemise.'

That also was taken off with alacrity, and she was before him perfectly naked. Heavens! What a sight! The whiteness of her skin, which shone like alabaster, the exquisite

114

contour of her limbs, and the tremulous motion which pervaded every muscle, formed a combination of lustful excitement that utterly baffles description.

He then ordered her to lie down on her back, raise her knees, and place her heels against her buttocks, then insert her finger in that divine cunt and frig herself.

She did so.

'How do you feel, darling? Are you going to spend? I will that you spend at once.'

Her whole body stiffened.

'Keep your thighs widely extended,' he said, 'so that I can see every throb that convulses your cunt, when the lovely liquor of love oozes forth.'

She obeyed, and with a deep sigh he saw it gush forth and cover her caressing hand.

He rushed forward and gamahuched her furiously, and then sitting in an easy chair, said, 'Ethel, get up.'

She obeyed, and following his commands, knelt in front of him, unfastened the front of his trousers, inserted her hand, and drew forth his prick; she then sucked it until with a positive howl of delight he inundated her mouth with his spendings. He then desired her to rise and kneel on the couch, then coming behind her he gently pulled apart the cheeks of her divine bottom, and disclosed the little orifice that lay nestling between them. This he sucked till he spent again, clasping her hips as he spent with spasmodic force.

He burned to fuck her, but dared not venture, and after a short time he ordered her to resume her clothes and then repeated the passes of a contrary direction until she recovered her senses, and to his great delight, she evidently knew nothing of what had taken place.

Mr and Mrs Etheridge had not returned when they reached the house, and they found a note stating that they were detained and could not be home till the following day.

On reading this Frank immediately remembered the proximity of his sister's bedroom and determined, at any risk, to gratify his intense desire with respect to her, this very night.

115

Before retiring he embraced her warmly, pressing her breasts against his chest and pushing his belly against hers; to his intense delight he felt her whole frame vibrate from the intensity of her emotion as her head fell on his shoulder.

He bade her good night and departed to his room.

As soon as he was convinced the house was quiet he gently opened his door and stole on tiptoe to his sister's room. To his intense delight it was unfastened.

He entered and saw his sister lying on her snowy bed, which was illumined by the rays of the moon.

She slept; he watched for some moments the rise and fall of her bosom, and the exquisite beauty of her face, and then commenced to mesmerize her again. She moaned faintly, and appeared restless.

'Sleep,' said he, and she immediately became quiet.

'Ethel,' he continued, 'do you know who is speaking to you?'

'Yes, my darling brother.'

He next pulled down the bed-clothes, and gently placed himself by her side, naked as he was.

'My darling,' said he, 'take off your night dress and chemise.'

She raised herself in the bed and did so, and then lay down again.

He clasped her in his arms, utterly intoxicated with his anticipated bliss.

The contact of her skin with his own, the knowledge that she was unconscious of what he was doing, and that it was his own sister, almost maddened him.

He was literally consumed with lust, and embraced her in every direction. Passing his arms between her thighs, he nestled his head on her divine belly. He next shifted it to her bosom, then he placed his prick between those firm and pouting breasts then between her thighs. He next placed his finger inside the lips of her cunt, and found to his surprise that it entered easily.

'Thank God,' he muttered, 'she has been frigged, possibly fucked, and I shall not hurt her.'

116

He willed her to take his prick and insert it in that divine recess, and to his intense joy he succeeded in burying himself in her with scarcely any difficulty.

He then lay powerless, and the spasm overtook him and ebbed forth into the inmost recesses of his sister's cunt.

He lay for a few moments in a profound lethargy, when he suddenly found his sister's cunt contracting and throbbing around his prick, which was still soaking within her. This fired him, anew, and placing both hands beneath her buttocks, he pressed her cunt towards him with the utmost force, while driving in and out of her with deep and body-killing thrusts. They both spent simultaneously, and after a short pause he arose and contemplated her, then willing her to resume her night dress and chemise, he returned to his own room, fearing that he might fall asleep and be discovered in the morning.

As he lay down he noticed a ray of light in a dark corner of his room, and on examining the panelling, found that a crevice existed through which he could see perfectly into his sister's room. There she still lay slumbering peacefully, and it suddenly struck him that he had forgotten to awaken her from the magnetic sleep which evidently still overpowered her.

He immediately commenced the necessary process and, to his delight, found that it had the same effect, nothwith-standing the wall which intervened.

She rose in the bed, and altering her position, lay calmly and naturally.

He retired to bed again, but was restless and excited and could not sleep; his prick was still stiff, and every nerve throbbed.

He lay tossing about in this way for an hour or so, when he suddenly heard a sound of whispering in the next room, and on peeping through the crevice into his sister's apartment, beheld a sight that rendered him spellbound and breathless.

He saw on her bed a figure perfectly naked, and of the most exquisite form, rivalling that of Ethel herself. She was kneeling and in the act of pulling the clothes from his sister, and raising her night dress, gazed ardently at her cunt. 'How wet and sticky it is to-night, Miss. You must have had such a wet dream.'

The lovely stranger placed her fingers within it and rubbed them about in the moisture, and then substituted her tongue, sucking luxuriously the lips and clitoris, and thrusting in the velvet tip as far as it would go into the vagina, until Ethel murmured. 'It is coming again, Mabel. Oh! Oh! Suck harder, my dear.' He now recognised the stranger as a housemaid who had attracted his attention on more than one occasion during the short time he had been in the house.

His sister now sought Mabel's cunt, and inserting a finger, commenced pushing it backwards and forwards as she embraced her lovely buttocks with her disengaged arm, burying her tongue within the rosy bottom-hole.

They writhed like two serpents, their bodies arched, and they fell prone on each other, every muscle vibrating as they spent in all the agonies of lasciviousness.

Frank seized his prick and frigged himself in unison with their movements, spouting out a torrent of sperm at the same moment as the two lovely tribades lost consciousness in their blissful convulsions.

When he looked again Ethel had taken the housemaid across her knees, and was rubbing her belly and sucking her nipples, ever and anon allowing her hand to wander between her thighs. She then turned her with her belly downwards, so that their cunts were in contact, and again passing her hand between Mabel's thighs, she rubbed the profuse spendings with which their cunts overflowed into her exposed bottom-hole and then inserting her finger, pushed it in and out its entire length, while Mable struggled to release herself.

At length she succeeded, and the housemaid lay flat on her back with Ethel reversed above her, and the sound of their mutual sucking, as their heads were between each other's thighs, drove Frank almost to the verge of distraction.

They swayed to and fro, and pressed each other with their utmost strength, until it was evident they were spending again. Still the gamahuching continued, until they seemed utterly exhausted; and Mabel, kissing Ethel madly, left the room, evidently to return to her own before the other servants were stirring, as the day was already breaking.

Frank was utterly bewildered, but now determined that he would use his knowledge and ravish his darling sister without the aid of mesmerism before many days had passed.

Mr and Mrs Etheridge returned about midday, and Frank was again struck by his mother's rare beauty and the fullness of her magnificent bosom. He looked at her fixedly, and, strange to say, she seemed affected by his gaze much in the same manner as his sister had been at first.

Frank felt a thrill of delight as the bare possibility occured to him of revelling in his mother's charms, but he felt that if he ever did succeed the utmost caution would be necessary.

In the afternoon he took another stroll with his sister, and they soon found themselves in the summer house.

They sat side by side on the couch, and Frank warmly embraced her, pressing her to him with voluptuous energy. She looked into his eyes and breathed heavily. His hand roved down and pressed one cheek of her buttocks, which he felt undulate beneath her bottom.

'You must not do that,' she murmured, 'it makes me feel sick and ill.'

'Does it when Mabel does the same?' asked Frank.

She became white with terror.

'Do not fear, my darling,' continued Frank. 'I know all, have seen your embraces last night, but alluded to it to assure you your secret is safe. But will you not now allow me some little privileges?'

'Oh, my darling, you are my brother!'

'So much greater the exquisite enjoyment,' pleaded Frank.

Her head fell on his shoulder, and he ventured to

insinuate his fingers within the bosom of her dress and gently rubbed her nipples with his thumb and finger.

She shivered with delight.

He next proceeded to place her hand upon his trousers, so that she could feel his bursting prick beneath. She clutched it wildly. He now gently pushed her backwards and placed one hand beneath her clothes, gently pressing her legs and thighs apart, until he at length succeeded in reaching her cunt, which was in a moist and spending condition.

She tore open his trousers, saying, 'Oh! Darling, forgive me, I cannot help it,' and pushed the skin of his prick backwards and forwards.

Frank commencing to frig her at first gently, gradually increasing the rapidity and depth of his insertion, till, with a shriek of rapture, she spent profusely. He resisted the impulse to follow her example, and seating himself in a chair, drew her towards him, placed his knees between her thighs, and allowed her gradually to sit down, while his prick penetrated her.

They embraced madly, thrusting their tongues into each other's mouths, and even biting each other in the fury of their transports, until another emission relieved their feverish lubricity.

They then resumed their position on the couch, and Ethel burst into a flood of tears.

'Oh! My brother,' sobbed she, 'what have we done, and what will be the consequence?'

Frank strove to console her, and after a time succeeded, and she became calm, so that they could resume their walk and return to the house.

It is now time that some explanation should be offered as to the cause of the mesmeric power and voluptuous development so strikingly manifested in Frank.

When he first reached school in Germany he was perfectly innocent, but was speedily initiated into all the mysteries of frigging and prick sucking by his school-fellows, who also used to fuck each other between the thighs, while a third behind received the point of his prick in his mouth each time it was pressed forward and sucked out every drop of spend that he could obtain.

One day when passing one of the master's rooms, he peeped in and saw him making mysterious motions in front of a pale, senior boy, who was celebrated amongst his companions for the enormous size of his prick and balls.

He watched with curiosity, and saw the boy fall apparently asleep. The master then proceeded to divest him of his trousers, handling with evident delight the boy's private parts. He then tucked up his shirt under his waistcoat, leaving the whole of his belly, bottom, thighs, and his lovely prick exposed.

The master gazed with rapture, and Frank saw by the lump that suddenly appeared in his trousers that his cock was evidently standing erect and hard.

He then said, 'Kneel on that sofa, and lean your arms on the head of it, I will it!'

Frank was intensely surprised to see the boy obey as though he were walking in his sleep.

The master took from an adjacent cupboard a birch and went to the head of the sofa, then leaning over the prostrate form of the boy commenced to flog him with it on his bottom and the inside of his thighs, but not severely.

He next unbuttoned his own trousers, and out sprang his prick in a state of glorious development, skinned and hard.

Frank could scarcely resist the inclination to rush in and beg to be allowed to suck it, but he refrained from fear and also lest his curiosity as to what was about to take place should be baulked.

The master spoke to the boy, 'Raise your head, and take my prick in your mouth, and suck it till I spend.'

The victim complied in the same mechanical manner.

The birching was now resumed, and as the master's excitement increased the blows fell heavier, the boy's bottom becoming red and inflamed.

He also commenced fucking the boy in the mouth, pushing himself backwards and forwards, when suddenly

121

he dropped the birch, and seizing the boy's head forced his prick within his mouth as far as he could ram it, spent, saying with spasmodic gasps, 'Swallow it all – my – spunk – shall – go down – your throat – if it – kills you.'

When he withdrew his reeking cock, the spend was glistening in and around the boy's lips, but he had most undoubtedly swallowed nearly all but a few drops.

The master now came to the side of the sofa, and passing his hand beneath the boy's belly, felt his lovely prick, but it was not stiff. He separated the thighs a little, and tickled his testicles, still it would not stiffen. He then skinned it, and stooping took the head between his lips. This had no better effect. He again commenced to birch him, stopping for a moment to rub his testicles and prick with eau de cologne.

The master's prick was again furiously erect, so throwing the birch down again he took a small pot of cold cream and produced an implement somewhat resembling an artificial prick (it was in fact a dildo), which he plentifully rubbed with the ointment, then taking more on his finger, approached the boy, and pressing apart the cheeks of his bottom, began to anoint the tight, wrinkled bumhole with it, gradually inserting his finger further and further inside. He then took the dildo, and applying it to the orifice, pushed it steadily in, until its entire length was buried in his anus; leaving it there he again examined the boy's prick, and was evidently delighted to find that at last it stood as stiffly as his own.

He then withdrew the dildo, and after rubbing his own prick with cold cream, knelt on the sofa behind the boy, and pointed the head of his cock at the well moistened orifice, pulling apart the buttocks with both hands, he eventually succeeded in penetrating the boy thoroughly. He next proceeded with both hands, which he passed in front of the boy's belly, and seized his glorious prick and balls, and while fucking him in the bottom, frigged him also, now stopping, and then again proceeding with rapidity, until at last the boy spent profusely, at the same moment that the master deposited within him his exhilarating emission.

Frank now passed on, fearing discovery, as the master had evidently finished for the present. He was puzzled at the mysterious manner in which the boy seemed to have been rendered insensible, and the fact of a great prick perforating a bottom-hole also filled him with astonishment.

He resolved to make the attempt to achieve this latter result with this very boy, who slept in his dormitory, and try what it was like. And it may be added that he successfully carried his project into effect the same evening, to the great surprise and extreme delight of the boy, who had knowingly been operated on in a similar manner, probably on many occasions.

Shortly after this he spoke of the extraordinary power one being seemed to possess over another, making them unconscious, and then compelling them to obey their orders.

This was to a young student at a neighbouring college, with whom he had become intimate, even to the extent of frigging each other. This friend explained the theory and practice of mesmerism, and Frank soon found that he could also experimentalize successfully.

This young student was also an ardent voluptuary of the most pronounced type, and proposed that Frank should try if he could mesmerize his sister, a charming girl of about sixteen, who was staying with him for a few days, awaiting the arrival of her father. Frank's friend proposed they should go to a certain house, where he was in the habit of going, to try the experiment. It was, in fact, kept by a lady who allowed the strangest scenes of unbridled lust to be enacted there, the contemplation of which caused her the most exquisite delight.

They started at once, in company with his friend's sister, and on their arrival the lady ushered them into her drawing room (fully understanding that their visit was to afford her some of the usual voluptuous treats, which she always enjoyed so much), and Frank at once commenced to try his experiment on the Fräulein.

For some time no visible effect was produced, but at last

123

her eyes appeared to dilate, then the eye-lids drooped, and she seemed to sleep.

'Now, Frank,' said his friend, 'speak to her.'

He did so, and to his delight he found that he had succeeded perfectly.

The student now told Frank that he must see him fuck her.

He started in amazement.

'Why she has never been touched! And I have never seen her cunt!'

'So much the better sport,' replied his friend, 'for I am determined you shall defile her in my presence here.'

'Now, Frank,' continued he, placing his hand on his prick and commencing to fondle it, 'no one but ourselves can ever know anything about it. I am so anxious to see her naked body, and this darling prick penetrating it. I see you will,' said he as he felt the cock rising under his caressing hand.

Frank was ready for anything. He approached her, unfastened her dress, discovering her rosy nipples tipping the snowy hills of her bosom. He fingered them in rapture, and they seemed to get so impudently hard that he could not resist the temptation of sucking the delicious little strawberries of love. But, his friend getting impatient, he proceeded to raise her dress in front, exhibiting a lovely little pink cunt, with scarcely a hair on it.

'I will assist you to undress her,' said the brother, and lifting her on the couch she was soon naked in their hands.

Frank examined that deliciously tight little cunt; it was impossible to get even the point of his finger in.

'How can I fuck this?' said he.

'Nonsense!' said the brother. 'Suck it and moisten it.'

Frank did so, and from the writhing of the naked body of the beautiful girl, she was evidently enjoying it. Her brother then took his place and endeavoured to force his tongue within. At last he arose, and said, 'Frank, I fear you must place your prick between her thighs and spend there, she is so small and tight, and I will suck the head of your prick

124

from the other side.'

This was carried into effect, and after commanding her to dress, Frank succeeded in recovering her again, and they left the house.

This little incident had created in Frank's mind a mad desire to force his way into a virgin cunt, he revelling in the agony of his victim by anticipation, and on mentioning his desire to his friend, he said, 'I will speak to a lady that I know very well.'

This was the proprietress of the house they had visited with his sister. She had a girl of eighteen of French parentage who had been turned out of her home by brutal parents and was, in fact, utterly friendless.

Madame G——— had taken her in with delight, seeing that she would be able to do anything with her that her lewd fancies might devise, without fear or risk.

This was the victim fated to be tortured by Frank, the only condition being that Madame G——— should be present to see the whole proceeding, and thus have her share of the voluptuous feast.

On the following day Frank obtained permission to be absent until evening, and he accompanied his friend to the house in question.

They were ushered into a charming boudoir, where they found Madame G——— awaiting them. She was a pretty, plump woman, every feature betraying an intensely lascivious temperament. She was completely enveloped in a dressing gown of black velvet, which heightened the dazzling whiteness of her skin; her rosy little feet were encased in tiny little slippers, and her legs were evidently bare.

A soft warm air pervaded the room, and a fragrant and exciting perfume shed its influence around. The floor was covered with a thick velvet pile carpet; the chairs and a capacious couch were also covered with velvet and furnished with luxurious springs. In the centre of the room was a peculiar article of furniture, which bore the appearance of a St Andrew's Cross, placed horizontally and supported by a massive pedestal, which at one end was cut away so as to correspond with the form of the cross at its lower extremity.

She rose and greeted them, embracing both most affectionately, and squeezed Frank so ardently against her that his prick stood immediately. Finding this to be the case she took his hand and placed it beneath her dressing gown; he shuddered on discovering that it was the only article that concealed her nakedness.

He pressed her belly amorously, and placing his hand at the junction of her thighs, discovered a most exquisite cunt and a clitoris erect and hard. She would not allow him to proceed further, as she only wished to see if he was sufficiently excited for the work he was intended to perform.

All sitting down, they partook of some Burgundy and literally devoured a collection of books, photographs, and pictures she had placed before them. They were of the most fearfully exciting character, representing lust and cruelty in every phase; the principal works being the Marquis de Sade's *Justine* and *Juliette*, in ten volumes, with their one hundred steel plates, also his *Philosophie dans le Boudoir* and other French works, besides English erotic books, such as *Fanny Hill*, *The Romance of Lust*, *Letters from Paris*, *Curiosities of Flagellation*, *Phoebe Kissagen*, *The New Epicurean*, and others too numerous to be mentioned.

When she saw they were both half frantic, she rose and rang the bell. In a few moments the door opened, and a remarkably beautiful girl entered.

'Sit down,' said Madame G———, 'I wish to speak to you.'

She obeyed, evidently frightened at the sight of two strange young gentlemen.

Madame then locked the door, and placing the key on the mantelpiece, turned to their victim.

'Marie,' said she, addressing the girl, 'these two handsome young fellows are going to fuck you. Do you know what that means?'

126

The poor girl began to sob, and trembled from head to foot.

'Oh! Madame,' said she, 'have mercy! I am so terrified – pray let me go!'

'No,' thundered her tormentor, 'I will not. Your screams cannot be heard beyond this room, and I intend to gloat over your ecstasy, while you are pleasured by all here. Seize her,' she added, addressing Frank and his friend, who were evidently influenced by the same feelings of ungovernable lust.

They sprang up and held her fast.

'Undress her.'

This they endeavoured to do, but her struggles were such that they could not succeed.

Madame G——— now approached, and seizing her arms, held them as in a vise, and directed Frank's friend to hold her legs. Frank then tore open her dress, and throwing her on the floor, they succeeded by their joint endeavours in tearing it completely off. She was forcibly divested of her stays, petticoats, drawers, stockings, everything in fact, till at last she lay on the floor struggling and screaming in a perfectly nude condition.

'Lift her on the cross table,' said Madame.

And with some difficulty they succeeded in extending their victim on her back, with her legs and arms stretched out on the four branches of the cross, and securely fixed in that position by concealed springs.

There lay her lovely naked form, every muscle convulsed by fear and outraged modesty.

Madame G——— then proceeded to suck her breasts and rub her belly and the inside of her thighs, directing Frank to fondle her cunt. This he obeyed delightedly, and then proceeded to suck it, causing her to struggle more and more, as in spite of all her fear and the shock to her modesty she was becoming excited, and in a few moments gave down a most copious spend.

This was the signal madame was waiting for. 'Now,' she exclaimed, 'your maidenhead shall be broken through – lost and destroyed!'

Frank and his friend stripped themselves to the buff, Madame also throwing off her only garment.

Acting on her instructions. Frank approached the lower end of the cross table, and placed himself between the victim's legs, placed the point of his prick just within the lips of her spending cunt, his friend taking up his station at the other end of the table with his rampant fiery cock just above the horrified face.

Madame, for her part, knelt on a prie-dieu, from the back of which protruded a dildo, which immediately entered her ready cunt to the very hilt, and leaning forward she recommended sucking and biting the tender nipples of her victim.

Frank now gave a swift lunge, and excited to madness by the shrieks of outrage and helpless struggles of the poor girl, was buried in her in a moment, his impatient prick breaking or tearing through every maiden obstacle, till the virgin blood trickled over his testicles and down the crack of her bottom.

His friend now commenced to frig himself, and Madame G——— was also pushing furiously · backwards and forwards on the dildo, as Frank now fucked the girl with deep and agonizing insertions of his prick.

The victim fainted from excess of pain and emotion, seeing which, Madame violently bit her bosom, and she recovered consciousness with a shriek of anguish, just as Frank spent within her abused body, and his friend inundated her face with the spunk that poured from his spending prick. at the same time Madame covered her dildo also with a prolific emission. This only increased the frenzy of her tormentors, and springing to their feet they eagerly agreed to Madame's suggestion to flog her.

Having reversed their victim so that she now lay on her belly, with a concealed dildo of immense size forcing itself up her cunt, they proceeded with three sturdy birch rods to carry this into effect, lashing her bottom, loins, inside her thighs, and even the lips of her cunt, tightly distended around the huge dildo, till the hue of her skin was a burning scarlet.

Then desisting, Madame G—— took another dildo, and pulling wider apart the cheeks of that smarting bottom, eased it into her convulsed and tender bottom-hole with some force.

The victim's tortures were almost too great for human endurance.

'Now,' Madame exclaimed, with the wild glare of a demoniac. 'I will sit astraddle her waist, and Frank must do so also, facing me.'

This was immediately carried into effect, Frank's prick entered the cunt in front of him with the greatest ease. Their violent up and down motions caused the dildo buried in the cunt of the almost crushed victim to fuck her.

'Faster, faster,' shrieked Madame G——. 'I'm coming – I'm coming – I'm spending!'

Their movements were fast and furious, and just as their spunk flowed with convulsive throbs, Frank's friend slapped hard the quivering buttocks of the victim, causing the most exquisite torture.

She moaned piteously, but this only excited her tormentors' devilish lusts to a greater extent, and joining each other on the couch, they enacted every device of lasciviousness.

They sucked and frigged, spending over each other in every direction. Then getting up, Frank withdrew the dildo from the bottom-hole of the suffering girl, substituted his prick, which was slippery with spendings, and commenced to fuck her there, whilst his friend inserted his under one of her extended arms, so that the point rubbed against one of the nipples of her bosom.

Madame G——, not to be behind hand, again seated herself astraddle the victim's waist, and rubbing her opened cunt in the spendings that still remained on her back from the previous fucking that had taken place there, frigged herself thus, as Frank increased her excitement and pleasure by working his moistened fingers in the wrinkled bumhole she presented to his view, to her intense enjoyment.

They all spent at the same time, even the victim, who could not resist the effect of the dildo still within her cunt. She was now literally inundated with spunk, and utterly exhausted, as the others resumed their clothes.

It can easily be imagined that this extraordinary adventure corrupted Frank Etheridge's mind, and his madly lascivious temperament is no longer a matter of surprise to the reader.

To return to our story. A few days after Frank and Ethel had knowingly fucked. Mr and Mrs Etheridge were obliged to visit London, and the brother and sister resolved to utilise the occasion.

Frank, during the interim, had succeeded in gamahuching and fucking the housemaid who had visited his sister in her room on that memorable night.

He had prevailed on his sister to have her as a bedfellow, and enact every species of exciting lust and tribadism they could devise.

This was carried into effect, and Frank, from his post of observation at the crevice, saw them perfectly naked, lying on the outside of the bed, the housemaid being reversed above her mistress, while they were literally devouring each other's cunts.

He then descended, and softly entering the room, naked as he was, made a sign to his sister. She instantly clutched the body of the housemaid above her, so that she could not extricate herself from the position she was in.

Frank now approached; and having previously applied oil plentifully to his prick, he knelt over his sister's face, and with a sudden thrust forward, buried it within the bottom-hole of the astonished housemaid.

She screamed in alarm, but Ethel, raising her thighs, literally buried the girl's head between them and effectually stifled her cries.

Frank proceeded to push his prick in and out, as he

130

revelled in this charming aperture, while his sister, abandoning for a moment the delicious cunt she was sucking, took his slippery balls in her mouth and rolled her tongue around them in such an exciting manner that he spent immediately, his spunk oozing out and flowing over the face of his delighted sister.

Mabel also emitted at the same moment, so that Ethel was almost choked.

Mabel was now ready enough to join in whatever they wished, and every species of ingenuity conceivable was brought into requisition, in order to minister to their mutual gratification.

At last Frank retired to his own room, sleeping soundly till late in the morning, when he awoke with such an awful cockstand and such a feeling of insatiable lust that he could scarcely put his prick out of sight in his trousers and make a decent appearance at the breakfast table.

He easily persuaded his sister to join him in a warm bath, which Mabel was ordered to prepare at once, and then when they had entered it she was to lock herself in Ethel's bedroom so that the other servants might not by any accident discover what was taking place.

Entering the bath, they lay down side by side, and an exquisite feeling of languor overtook them.

Ethel's hand wandered over her brother's naked form beneath the water, and his was not idle.

Then rising, they stood facing each other, and slightly extending her thighs, her brother speedily placed his erect and throbbing prick within her. They commenced to fuck gently, fondling each other as they did so.

The convulsive spasms, however, speedily approached, and at the moment they mutually commenced to spend they sank down in the warm water. The beautiful warmth of the aromatic bath produced most delicious sensations flowing up their buttom-holes, as busy fingers worked excitedly to increase their lascivious abandon, while its action around their still more sensitive organs of generation caused them heavenly rapture.

131

The day before the return of their parents, Frank and Ethel were seated in the summer house mutually fondling each other's private parts, when Frank said that the desire he had long felt to see his mother's glorious nakedness, and if possible to fuck and gamahuche her, grew stronger every day, and he was resolved to try it by the aid of mesmerism.

Ethel, blushing deeply, was evidently much excited by the idea, and confessed that the same feelings with respect to her father had possessed her for some time.

'Then, my darling,' continued her brother, 'we will do it.'

Mabel now entered, and stopped further conversation by frigging herself before them, while they also performed the same act for each other, after which they all returned to the house.

Mr and Mrs Etheridge arrived the next day about one o'clock. They embraced their children with great warmth, but little imagined the libidinous feelings their endearments produced on their children.

It will be well, before relating what subsequently took place, to glance at Ethel's school experiences, in order to understand her lustful desires and warm temperament.

The school in Paris at which she was placed was conducted by a lady of tall stature, Juno-like form, and a manner which, outwardly mild, concealed beneath it the fire of raging lust, which she gratified in a peculiar manner.

She received Ethel most kindly, and kissing her affectionately, consigned her to the care of a young lady some three or four years older, who would be her special companion and share her bed.

She was afterwards introduced to the other young ladies, and at once felt thoroughly at home.

When they retired for the night, Ethel's companion, Minette, insisted on helping her to undress, and although from a natural feeling of shyness Ethel did not like it much, she did not wish to appear ill-natured or ungrateful, so she permitted it.

132

Minette managed in this operation, apparently by accident, to bring her hands in contact with Ethel's naked body as much as possible, which caused blushes to mantle her face, as she felt the contact of the soft, pulpy hand.

Ethel now got into bed, having first rendered similar assistance to Minette, who did not possess the shyness of her younger friend, but before putting on her nightdress completely bared her whole body before the eyes of Ethel, who was somewhat surprised to see such large prominent breasts and a profusion of hair covering her cunt.

She immediately embraced Ethel on getting into bed and endeavoured to interlace their legs, which somewhat surprised the new pupil, and made her keep them close together, not knowing the meaning of such proceedings.

Before sleeping they lay apart, and Ethel, tired out as she was, speedily sank into a refreshing slumber.

She dreamt that every portion of her body was pervaded by the most delicious sensations, but could not conceive the cause, and when she awoke in the morning was surprised to find one of Minette's hands between her thighs, whilst another rested on her little breasts.

Her companion was asleep, or pretended to be so, and was entirely uncovered, the bed-clothes having slipped off. She was lying on her back, her legs widely extended, and her cunt moist, slightly open and occasionally twitching with a spasmodic throb, whilst she sighed gently and smiled in her sleep.

Ethel was possessed by a nameless sensation, and actuated by curiosity, ventured to look closer at the full-blown cunt, which seemed to rivet her gaze, and saw a little fleshy lump protruding from between the luscious-looking vermillion lips.

Struck with amazement, as she herself had nothing of the kind, she touched it gently with her fingers. It throbbed, and Minette sighed slightly, and said, in a kind of subdued whisper, 'Oh, do go on, rub your finger about, my darling Clara, it is so exquisite!'

She was evidently asleep, and imagined someone else was

with her.

Ethel, hardly knowing what she was about, commenced to rub the little lump, and was surprised still more to find that Minette moved uneasily, opening and shutting her legs, till at last she heard a profound sigh, and Minette lay motionless.

Ethel felt a strange throbbing, and her finger was immediately wetted with a warm gush of thick creamy glutinous something which was emitted from the cunt of her bedfellow.

This so affected her that she withdrew her finger, and lay apart from her companion again.

Presently the sleeper awoke, and they dressed, Minette again insisting on various squeezings and fondlings, which now produced on Ethel a most strange effect, perfectly incomprehensible to her, whilst Minette seemed also intensely excited.

However, they descended to breakfast without any further adventure, except that another pupil, Mademoiselle Rosalie, a frolicsome blonde, handed Ethel on the sly a piece of poetry in English, which she pretended she could not read herself but which might perhaps interest 'la belle Anglaise.'

Ethel put the printed slip away in her bosom, and afterwards read at her leisure as follows, a very comical parody:

PITY THE SORROWS

(Parody on Pratt's 'Pity the Sorrows of a Poor
Old Man,' Annual Register 1770, page 222)

Pity the sorrows of a fat young wife,
 Whose youth and vigour make her pine the more!
Whose bounding pulse with hot desire is rife,
 O give relief, and heaven shall bless your store!

These rosy cheeks, my bursting youth bespeak,
 These beaming eyes proclaim my ardent quim,
But O! my husband is so cold and weak,

I might be dead, and buried too, for him!

My widow'd sister Mary pines like me,
　　But while he liv'd, her husband was a man!
My married sister Lucy smiles to see,
　　How oft I'm baffled since my hopes began!

I will not, cannot tell, for very shame,
　　All that is wanting to the married state,
To be a wife in nothing but the name,
　　Is a most wretched, miserable fate!

Though chaste in heart, and willing to be chaste,
　　What virtue can withstand the waltz's whirl?
Tom, Jack, or Harry's arm about my waist,
　　Belly to belly throbbing, boy with girl!

To sup on partridges and to drink champagne,
　　Stirs my hot blood to fever's ardent glow,
And then the waltzing round and round again,
　　Drives me quite mad! O what, what can I do?

I'd willingly be wise and chaste, God knows!
　　But O, it drives me wild with amorous pain,
To feel the embracing arms of waltzing beaux,
　　To meet the piercing glance of charming men!

O, tell me, have I err'd? Impart the truth!
　　My inmost heart is open to conviction,
Deeper, O deeper still, dear vigorous youth,
　　O, give me every inch of thine erection!

Pity the sorrows of a fat young wife,
　　All, all my sins are lying at your door,
Bestow on me the biggest joys in life,
　　Oh, give relief, and heav'n shall bless your store!

Our school-girl was more perplexed than ever by this effusion: what was that something always required by blooming
young wives or widows so mysteriously hinted at in the lines
as she read them over and over again to herself?

At the close of their morning studies Madame Cul addressed her pupils and stated that Mademoiselle Rosalie had not completed her French exercises to her satisfaction, and as she could not allow idleness and carelessness to exist in her establishment, she would be birched in the presence of the whole school after luncheon.

Ethel stared in amazement, but Minette lovingly placed her arm round her waist and whispered, 'It is the custom here, but you will soon get used to it, and even enjoy the sight.'

According, before the commencement of afternoon studies, Madame Cul entered the schoolroom, followed by two well-formed but muscular and strong housemaids, and when all were assembled, said, 'Mademoiselle Rosalie, come here and take off everything except your chemise, shoes and stockings. The maids will assist you to do so.'

The poor girl advanced tremblingly, for she had not long entered the establishment, and this was but her second birching.

When she was divested of her dress Madame Cul directed one of the housemaids to assist her in getting on the other one's back, where she was securely held by the hands, the servant acting as horse, having her firmly gripped by each wrist, whilst the other strong young woman was directed to hold the victim's legs well apart.

Ethel gazed as if fascinated by the pretty and luscious sight presented to her view; it was so exciting to see Rosalie, who was about sixteen, with an exquisitely fair complexion, her face flushed with shame, with deep blue eyes brimful of tears, just ready to run down the crimson cheeks, as Madame Cul raised first her skirts, which brought to view the poor girl's pretty legs, dressed in most interesting boots white silk stockings, and delicately trimmed drawers.

The poor girl seemed to quiver all over with emotion, as she first sobbed and then cried for mercy in a most piteous broken voice, 'Oh, Madame, do pray punish me in private as you did at first. Ah, no, no! I can't bear the shame of their all seeing my poor naked bottom.'

'Silly girl, hold that whimpering noise, you deserve all

this disgrace, did I not tell you how I would punish you before the whole school next time?' said Madame, evidently with some excitement, as she opened the girl's drawers behind, and pinned up the tail of her chemise with all the rest of the impedimenta round the victim's waist, till at last they had a very fair view of Rosalie's lovely little pink-lipped cunt, upon which the incipient growth of soft down was only just beginning to be perceptible, and another delightful item displayed to view was her tight wrinkled little bum-hole, set in a frame of soft-tinted delicate brown, beautifully in contrast with the snowy whiteness of the well-developed buttocks.

Madame now raised the birch with which she was provided, and commenced to lash the bottom so invitingly exhibited, increasing the severity of her cuts as she went on. Then resting a little she seemed to watch with much satisfaction the wriggling of the fair penitent, the cheeks of whose bottom were a fiery red.

When she recommenced, the birching was directed to the inside of the victim's thighs, and even on the lips of that delicately pink little cunt, with light smart touches, evidently intended to inflame the parts rather than cut them up.

Rosalie, her dark eyes now full of sensuous humidity, her face burning scarlet, alternately sobbed and cried as she commenced afresh to struggle wildly, so that the servants with all their strength could scarcely hold the plunging victim.

Madame Cul stopped the punishment, and to Ethel's intense surprise, she saw Rosalie's bottom-hole open and shut, whilst the throbbing lips of her cunt emitted a thick, whitish-looking liquid, which oozed forth in spasmodic gushes.

'Enough! She spends, the lewd girl; it only shows the prurient ideas girls must have when my birching affects them in such a sensual manner. Fie for shame, Mademoiselle Rosalie, what have you done?' exclaimed Madame, as she sank into a chair and seemed ready to faint herself, whilst the humidity of her eyes seemed the very counterpart to that sensuous look in her victim.

Recovering herself in a few moments, she directed them to release Rosalie, and then left the room.

During this extraordinary scene Minette had placed her hand behind Ethel and squeezed the cheeks of her bottom, also endeavouring to force it between her thighs as well as she could, considering how the intervening dress hindered this operation. Nevertheless our innocent novice could not help opening her legs a little, and felt a strange indescribable sensation of pleasure.

The other girls were moving restlessly on their seats and, in fact, were using dildoes concealed under their drapery.

When Minette and Ethel retired for the night, the former complained of the heat, and suggested that they should sleep without any covering or night dresses, and by way of example got into bed in a state of perfect nudity.

Ethel, not wishing to be thought prudish or ill-natured, first extinguished the light, and then threw off her chemise. Joining her companion bed-fellow also quite naked, they embraced each other warmly and Minette, placing her hand on Ethel's bottom, forced their cunts together. She trembled from head to foot, but when Minette asked her to squeeze her in a similar manner, she did so at once, and did not resist the insertion of one of her fair thighs between her own.

Minette now kissed her furiously, thrusting her tongue into Ethel's mouth, causing her to feel the most extraordinary sensations.

'Ethel, my darling,' she said, 'what did you think of Rosalie's birching, has she not got an exquisite bottom and pussy? Was it not awfully exciting when it throbbed?'

At the same time she gently placed her hand on Ethel's cunt, and commenced to suck one of her nipples, whilst one finger was titillating her companion's incipient clitoris, which, although so small as to be scarcely visible, was tremendously sensitive to these tender and lascivious touches by such an experienced tribade.

138

'Oh, oh, pray don't, you make me feel so sick – so odd – I tremble all over – I can't say how I feel – and yet – yet –,' said Ethel in a whisper, hardly knowing what to do as she struggled to get away a little from her rude bedfellow.

This only excited Minette the more, as she held the young girl firmly in her embrace, redoubling her ardent caresses, which seemed to send such a thrill of exquisite warmth through Ethel's entire frame that she was powerless to resist such seducing endearments.

Minette was not slow to take advantage of her conquest. Reversing her position all of a sudden, she forced her head between Ethel's thighs and commenced to suck her cunt, plunging her amorous velvety-tipped tongue in as far as it would go, or biting the little clitoris in such a way that her companion was almost mad with a feeling she could not yet fully understand.

She again struggled to release herself, but it was in reality only a semblance of resistance – the last faint protest of her modest nature before thoroughly surrendering herself to all the voluptuous games of Minette.

At last her head fell back, her throbbing cunt was raised to meet those warm, loving kisses, and then for the first time in her life, she really spent – and fainted.

When she recovered she threw herself into Minette's arms, saying, 'Oh, I have indeed been in heaven. What did you do to make me feel so?'

Her bedfellow hastened to fondle her again, and before another hour had passed they were mutually frigging, gama-huching, and spending amid cries of delight. In fact, Ethel was thoroughly taught every pleasure possible to tribadism.

The following day another girl was birched in school, and at night Minette proposed to Ethel that they should go into the next dormitory, after the lights were extinguished, and see what was going on, as the birched girl slept there.

They did so, and Ethel stood spellbound.

Twelve of the senior girls aged about sixteen, were all lying in a confused heap on two of the beds that had been placed close together, and they were sucking, frigging, and

139

fucking each other with dildoes.

Minette rushed to the bed and speedily mingled with the spending mass of girlhood, whilst Ethel, utterly unable to resist the impulse, ran forward also to the birched girl and was soon sucking her cunt, whilst other girls sucked her nipples or excited her almost to madness by working their fingers in her sensitive bottom-hole. After exhausting themselves with every kind of lubricity, they returned to their own room.

The next morning Ethel felt so fatigued she could not complete the task assigned her in school.

As she was leaving for recreation Madame Cul called her to one side, and said: 'You have incurred punishment by your neglect, but as you are evidently in a rather nervous state, I will inflict it in my bedroom. Come to me immediately after afternoon studies.'

At the appointed time Ethel tremblingly sought Madame Cul's bedroom.

The schoolmistress, after locking the door, proceeded to assist her in removing all her clothes. When this was accomplished she directed her to lie on a velvet couch that was covered with cushions. This she did, and Madame Cul adjusted her in such a manner that while lying on her belly one of the velvet cushions lay between her extended thighs.

She now commenced to birch her with light stinging cuts that, although not apparently heavy enough to break or lacerate her delicate skin, had such a smarting effect that Ethel felt she must scream to relieve the pain. This was presently succeeded by a warm voluptuous glow that sent a tremor through her whole frame. She felt as though she wanted to pee, and yet that did not seem the reason of her strange sensations.

As the birching proceeded, Madame occasionally placed her hand on the bottom of the penitent, which tended so to increase Ethel's excitement that, wildly squeezing the cushion between her thighs, she spent copiously.

Madame, delighted to see what had happened, lifted her own skirts and with a few insertions of her finger produced the same result on herself.

When she had recovered she ordered Ethel to rise, then pretending to notice the moisture on the pillow, asked her what she had been doing.

Poor Ethel blushed scarlet, and looked awfully distressed.

'Come here, my darling,' Madame said, 'let me see what has been the matter with you,' and she took her across her knees, extending her on her back.

She examined her cunt, pressed and rubbed her belly, squeezed her nipples between her fingers till they grew quite impudently erect, inserted her finger in Ethel's cunt, and commenced to frig the agitated girl luxuriously, making her toss about in such ecstasy that, when spending again, Madame could scarcely hold her, so violent were her contortions.

(Madame's finger entered easily, but she made no remark, for she knew full well that the entrance had been forced by Minette's finger – which was, in fact, the case.)

After this Ethel was initiated into every means of procuring sensual pleasure that Sapphism could teach, but it was not until her return home, and the subsequent meeting with her brother, that she actually felt the real delight of a prick inside her (which no substitutes can ever equal), although she knew all that man could do unto her.

It will be seen, therefore, that by reason of her school experiences she was well prepared for any species of lechery which her brother might venture to propose.

In the course of a few days Mr Etheridge was compelled again to visit the neighbouring town where he would be detailed till the next day.

Thus the opportunity came at last for which Frank had been waiting. At dinner he plied his mother with Burgundy (of which she was very fond) to the greatest possible extent; without raising her suspicions, whilst he literally devoured her with his gaze.

Later in the evening, she sat in a large easy chair and

141

seemed to be getting drowsy. Frank said, 'As we shall scarcely require anything else tonight, may the servants go to bed, Mamma?'

She assented, and after the order had been given, Frank, looking triumphantly towards his sister, seriously commenced his attempt to mesmerize his own mother. At first she involuntarily resisted his efforts, but at length she succumbed, and as her head fell on her shoulder he openly made the necessary passes, and she speedily became entirely at his mercy.

'Now, Ethel,' said he, 'I will gratify my passion.'

He approached his mother. She was in evening dress and her lovely bubbies were half visible, and from the seminecumbent position in which she lay every outline of her form could be clearly seen.

Her son first carefully raised those deliciously firm bubbies completely above her dress, then sucking one motioned to his sister to do the same with the other.

Mrs Etheridge sighed slightly and slid further down in her chair.

Frank then knelt in front of her, and his sister helping him, they gradually raised their Mamma's dress in front, till they had a full view of the splendid legs and thighs of their maternal parent – the former cased in pink silk stockings, with the swelling thighs filling out her drawers and making them look deliciously tight. Placing his hand within the slit in front he pulled aside the chemise, and gently extending her legs to their widest, he placed her feet on two chairs, and they now had a full view of that glorious cunt from which they both had come. It was beautifully shaded with hair, not too large, and between the moist lips he saw her divine clitoris, hard and erect.

After gazing for a moment, he rubbed it gently with his finger. Mamma again sighed, and slid still further forwards. Now taking from his pocket a dildo (which he had previously charged), he gradually inserted it in his mother and pushed it gently backwards and forwards. The lips clung lovingly to it, his mother's breathing became hurried, her

142

bubbies heaved under the caressing fingers of her daughter, and with a tremendous spasm that convulsed every muscle of her body, she spent, just as Frank pressed the spring and injected the contents of the dildo into her. Immediately removing the instrument and substituting his tongue, he drained every drop of spend that she emitted.

While he was thus occupied Ethel had stretched herself on the floor, and having released his bursting cock, was receiving within her mouth the spendings of her brother.

After gloating for some time over the sight of his mother's relaxed cunt, he suddenly placed her legs over his shoulders and raised her body in such a manner that his prick was opposite her bottom-hole. He, after his sister had rubbed some of the spunk within its wrinkled orifice, prepared for an *enculade*. Ethel meanwhile was gamahuching her mother's delicious cunt and being frigged by her brother.

Gradually Frank pushed his way within his Mamma's delightful fundament, which contracted and throbbed upon his tremendously excited prick, so that he at once spent in an agony of lust. His sister, equally maddened by the thoughts of her brother's incest and the voluptuous workings of his fingers on the lips of her cunt and clitoris, also emitted at the same time with a scream of rapture.

Then not to be outdone by her brother she made him withdraw his prick, which remained enormously stiff, and literally devoured it with her lips, sucking every drop of spend, etc., which still oozed from the fiery-looking head of his affair, and then pointing it to that divine maternal cunt she made him plunge in there and fuck Mamma properly and thoroughly, whilst she was sucking and tickling his balls in order to increase his enjoyment.

'Mamma, dear,' said Frank, withdrawing his prick after another ecstatic spend, 'do you know what you are doing?'

She answered immediately, 'Yes, my darling children, your delicious fucking and gamahuching have made me feel all the delights of heaven itself.'

Yet her eyes were closed, and there was no doubt of her being still under the mesmeric influence.

'Is there anything else you would like, dear Mother?' asked Frank.

'I should like to suck my dear boy's prick, whilst Ethel frigs me again,' she murmured.

Frank at once presented his half-stiffened cock to his mother's lips; whilst Ethel, kneeling down between the maternal thighs, rolled her lascivious tongue in delight round that splendid clitoris and within the serrated nymphae which guarded the entrance to the temple of love, whilst her nose revelled amongst the beautiful *chevelure* of a most glorious *mons Veneris,* and inhaled all the sweet odours of that Cytherian region, which always has maddening effects on the votaries of gamahuching.

She was too occupied with her tongue to frig her mother's cunt, but postilioned her luxuriously with two fingers in her bottom-hole; Mamma all the while was sucking the prick and caressing the balls of her son, as he fucked her in the mouth.

At last they were too exhausted to carry their ideas any further for the time, and having wiped their mother and removed every trace of her defilement – and allowed a little time for the blood to cool in their veins – she was placed in her former position in her chair, her dress readjusted, and then Frank, with a few passes, brought her back to consciousness, after which they all soon retired to rest.

The following day at lunch time Mr Etheridge returned home; but Mrs Etheridge did not appear, having a severe headache, doubtless (although she knew it not) the result of the operations of her children on her body the previous evening.

It was a lovely afternoon, and Mr Etheridge proposed a walk, to which his children readily assented.

After strolling about for upwards of an hour they directed their steps to the summer house, of which mention has been before made.

Both Frank and Ethel had been more than usually affectionate in their manner to their father this particular afternoon, and the latter had more than once brushed accidentally with the back of her head against the front of her father's trousers, and on the last occasion distinctly felt his prick, which was evidently in a slightly turgid state, and his trousers also slightly projected in the most interesting place.

Ethel's breath shortened and her voice was slightly thick and husky with a strange tremulousness in its tone, as she felt a curious and unnatural sensation stealing over her that she could not define even in her own thoughts.

Frank also seemed strangely excited, and occasionally pressed his sister's bubbies behind his parent's back. He also took every opportunity of pressing against his father.

When they sat down to rest Ethel noticed that her father appeared drowsy, and he lay down on the couch. Presently his eyes closed, and he seemed in a deep sleep. On looking towards her brother she saw he was making the mesmeric passes with his hands.

In a few moments he rose, and approaching his sister, said, 'My darling, Papa is now entirely unconscious of what he does, and entirely under my control; we will secure the door, and then you shall suck the author of your being till his noble prick spends in your mouth.'

He appeared almost mad, and Ethel remained for the moment almost spellbound – her feelings were too much for her.

'Now, Ethel,' continued her brother, 'you can do what you wish, do not lose time!'

Aroused by his words, she approached her father and knelt down by the side of the couch. He was lying on his back, with his thighs slightly separated. Taking hold of his legs she gently extended them still further, and his prick could be seen reposing on his left thigh.

Ethel tremblingly unfastened the buttons from waist to fork; then, gently removing his shirt, she saw before her her father's lovely prick. It was an exquisite object, purely white, streaked with delicate blue veins, the loose skin almost covering the head of it. His balls were hanging gracefully beneath, and fine silky hair surrounded the whole of his privates.

She touched the prick, and even ventured to place her fingers round it; and as she did so its substance increased. She gently pushed the skin up and down, it throbbed and grew harder and stiffer every moment, till at last it was proudly erect, standing against his spotless belly, as white as ivory and as hard as a bar of iron.

She lay her cheek lovingly on his thigh and kissed the point of it, and then took it between her lips, while with her fingers she tickled his balls, which were now hard and tight in their receptacle.

Frank now knelt behind his sister, and having raised her clothes, he separated her legs and soon ascertained that her cunt was delightfully moist and hot. Bringing his prick to the mark, he slowly inserted it, and then pushed gently backwards and forwards.

His sister took more of the paternal priapus in her mouth, and pushing her head to and fro, frigged it deliciously by the double action of her lips and tongue. She grew more and more excited in her gamahuching as the motions of Frank's prick stirred all the lubricity of her nature, till suddenly Mr Etheridge's lips parted with a deep-drawn sigh, the muscles of his belly hardened, and he spent in the mouth of his daughter, who also simultaneously received her brother's balmy emission in her cunt.

As the spending prick left the mouth of the gamahucher, Frank, withdrawing, took his sister in his arms, and thrusting his tongue into her mouth, they greedily enjoyed their father's spendings with which it was filled, as their hands mutually groped each other's prick and cunt.

Papa still lay on his back, his prick moist and glistening. Frank now seized the limp affair of his parent, and bringing his person close to his father, rubbed the head of the parental prick against that of his own. This immediately stiffened him again, and Frank directed Ethel to stand on the couch with her legs straddled over her father. She gradually stooped till the point of the great and glorious prick was at the entrance to her cunt, then with Frank's assistance it was guided into the lustful gap, she stooping lower and lower, till it penetrated her to the quick.

Her brother placed his hands under the cheeks of her bottom and jumped her up and down, till he saw by the contraction of his father's balls, and the immense increase of stiffness in the shaft of his prick, that he was about to spend again. Then he placed his head between his sister's thighs behind and with his tongue licked his father's balls and the lips of his sister's cunt, frigging himself at the same time.

When father and daughter spent, their joint spendings oozed out over his face and drove him frantic with enjoyment; then lifting his sister down, he made her suck his prick, which had just emitted, till it was stiff again, and then placing her on the floor he fucked her savagely, to her great delight in the excited state she then was, while he also frigged his father's cock till it came again in a copious spend.

They now removed all traces of what had happened; Frank then willed his father to awake, which he did. And looking round vacantly, he said, 'Dear children, I fear I have been to sleep, the fresh air does tire me so,' as he little thought of the real reason of his peculiar feelings of fatigue.

Frank, now perfectly sure that father, mother and sister were entirely amenable to his influence, was determined to gratify his lusts to the full, and with the aid of Ethel he counted on carrying out his intentions.

In addition to gratifying their licentious appetites in the manner already related, they also sought new excitements by utilizing certain animals on the farm. Ethel would frig a bull or a goat, and when milking a favourite cow, would suddenly persuade Frank to lift her in his arms, where she would lay extended on her back, and raising her clothes, would frig herself with the cow's teats, the milk from which would flow into her ravenous cunt to be afterwards sucked out by her brother.

Frank would also stealthily approach a goat and raise the animal's hind legs; Ethel would put cold cream on its cunt for him and insert her brother's prick, who would then, utterly regardless of the cruelty he inflicted, force his cock in and spend there.

At last another idea occurred to them.

They were sitting after dinner when Frank quietly mesmerized both father and mother and then asked Ethel to dismiss the servants for the night.

They amused themselves by playing with their parents' private parts for awhile, and then Frank willed them to go to their bedroom. This they immediately did. Brother and sister left them for a short time, retiring to their own rooms, and returned quite naked.

Their parents now mechanically divested themselves of every article of clothing, in obedience to the will of their son, whilst Frank also willed the housemaid Maud to come into the room naked. This girl, under his influence, first approached Mrs Etheridge and sucked her bubbies, then her cunt till she spent, after which she did the same with the prick of her master, while Frank and Ethel gamahuched her bottom-hole and cunt to stimulate her lasciviousness; then she was sent back to her room.

Mr and Mrs Etheridge began to fondle, and after struggling a little together on the bed, Mamma was pulled onto her husband, and they commenced a most luscious St George.

Heavens! What a sight for their incestuous son and daughter! With greedy eyes and bated breath, they watched that lovely prick appear and disappear within the loving cunt above it. Now the paroxysm of spending approached, and their voluptuous furor increased – it was simply maddening.

Frank and Ethel rushed forwards and with their hands assisted their beloved parents to experience the utmost possible enjoyment attainable, which they undoubtedly did, literally screaming with pleasure, as the spunk came forth in prolific streams.

Frank now determined to run a great risk in allowing his parents to know what was going on.

First directing his sister to lie on her back on the bed,

with extended thighs, he willed his father to lie on her and himself placed his prick within her cunt. Then his mother (under his influence) lay on her back, on the bed by Ethel's side, and Frank, excitedly mounting upon her, buried his prick within the moist and juicy folds of the delicious cunt that gave him birth.

As they were all four approaching the divine climax, Frank dissolved the mesmeric charm and allowed both father and mother to realise the situation at a moment when it would be impossible for them to resist the impulses of their carnal nature.

Mr Etheridge gave a cry of horror, and Mamma screamed with fright, but Ethel held her father in a convulsive embrace, her erotic fury making her at the moment as strong as a lioness, whilst Frank for his part thrust so vigorously at his mother that, in spite of their horror at the incestuous situation, they all spent simultaneously.

It would be impossible to describe the sense of shame that overcame the poor parents; they seemed to think they were still under the influence of some horrible dream, an idea which their children did their best to foster, whilst they were delighted by the sight of their father's fine prick stiffening again of itself, from the mere thought of having enjoyed his daughter.

Presently Ethel and her brother glided noiselessly from the room, but remained just outside the door to peep and listen. In a moment or two Mr Etheridge threw himself upon his wife in a perfect transport of lust, exclaiming, 'What a dream to fancy I've been fucking Ethel, and what joys she gave me! I feel, dear, as randy as if I had been away from you for six months!'

'How curious,' sighed Mrs Etheridge, 'that I am also excited by having been dreaming the same thing about dear Frank! Ah, how fine, stiff, and hot your love of a prick is, my dear, and as moist as if you had really had the girl. Put it into me quick, love, and I'll fancy you really are Frank. I'm excited enough to do the real thing at this moment!'

'For shame, wife,' responded Mr Etheridge, 'it's an awful

sin even to think about, and yet they do say the great Napoleon used to fuck his own sisters and aunts, and considered he had a right to enjoy himself as he pleased.'

'Besides,' continued Mrs Etheridge, 'there's the case of Lot and his daughters, and no doubt they were thought quite as respectable as ever by their acquaintances afterwards. In fact, they must have told about it for Moses to have known how to write the tale, and he could not have been very horrified at the incest, as he makes no mention of its being discontinued by Lot when he found it out. And then, you know, the ancient kings of Egypt always preferred to marry their mothers or sisters.'

Further remarks were stopped by the necessities of their amorous combat, so brother and sister retired, fully satisfied that their parents would soon be as easy as themselves with regard to incestuous intercourse with their children.

Next day Mr and Mrs Etheridge appeared greatly distressed and hardly able to look Frank and Ethel in the face, but in the course of a few days this all wore off. The equanimity returned, and whether owing to the mysterious influence of mesmerism or otherwise, they afterwards willingly enacted every species of licentiousness with their own children.

One day Frank and Ethel related to their parents their experiences at college and school. Mr Etheridge was so inflamed at the tale of the professor sodomizing the boy with the big prick that he declared he should never rest until Frank had procured him the same pleasure.

'Let me see,' he said, 'if I can think of a handsome, finely developed youth, who we can invite here some day for you to experimentalize upon. Yes, there's young Harry Mortimer. He has got a fine looking lump in his trousers – a perfect Adonis – I've often longed to handle his cock.'

'You old sinner,' laughed his wife, 'I always thought you a strictly moral man. And to think your ideas ever ran in such a beastly course. I, too, must confess, now Frank's mesmerism has made us all free with one another, how hard it has often been for me to retain my reputation as a chaste wife. Why there's Dr Stroker, our rector, who has tried me dozens of times, and once actually showed me his fine tool when we were alone in the drawing room. What a beauty it was! I almost fainted with desire.'

'Ah,' said Ethel, 'that's nothing to what he did with me, when I had to go to the rectory to prepare for confirmation. I was always alone with him. He used to laugh and tell me that religion was all humbug, he himself only followed and preached it as his trade, to get a good living. He would draw me on his lap, put his hands up my clothes, and tell me my cunny would soon have a crop of beautiful soft hair on it. And one day he threw me back and kissed my cunt till I fainted, and when I came round my clothes were up to my waist, and he was standing between my legs as they hung over the side of the sofa and frigging himself so as to spend all over my belly, and after all would not let me go till I had kissed and handled his cock. That was just before you sent me off to Madame Cul's school and no doubt all helped to make Minette's touches so awfully exciting when she began to seduce me with her wanton games.'

'Well have a game with him, Frank, my boy!' exclaimed Mr Etheridge. 'My idea now is that we may all do what we like to enjoy ourselves, only damn all jealousy. I'm a regular Communist now! Well, when I ride out tomorrow I will call and ask Harry to spend an early day with you.'

'Have you found anything worth reading to us yet, Frank?' asked his Mamma.

'Yes, a little bit about the quarrels of the goddesses in heaven. It is an old volume of the writings of the "London Spy." Here it is,' said Frank, taking up a book:

POEM

A health Jove began to the best end of Juno,
By which they had often been 'Junctus in Uno,'
The bowl went about with much simp'ring and winking,
Each God lick'd his lips, at the health he was drinking;
Whilst Venus and Pallas look'd ready to rave,

That her Goddesship's scut should such preference
    have;
The bowl being large, hoping the rather
Their amiable rumps might have swam altogether.
Thus both being vex'd, Venus swore by her power,
The nectar had something in't, made it drink sowre:
Which Pallas confirm'd by her shield and her sword,
And vow'd 'twas as musty besides as a T——d
But Juno perceiving 'twas out of ill-nature,
That Venus and Pallus abus'd the good creature,
Because to her Peacock, precedence was given,
As the best and finest fledg'd bird in the Heaven;
Insinuating under a wink and a snicker,
As if the good health had corrupted the liquor:
And finding they'd cast this reflection upon her,
In Juno 'twas justice to stand by her honour:
Who raising her bum from her seat in a passion,
To Venus and Pallas she made this oration:
'Pray Goddesses! What do you mean, I beseech it,
To basely reflect on my Tippet-de-wichet?
I know by your smiles, leering looks, and your winks,
And your items and jeers, you'd insinuate it stinks:
Dispraising the nectar, well knowing you meant,
That a health to my Tw——t gave the juice an ill scent.
Nay, laugh if you please, for I know I'm extreamly
To blame, thus to blurt out a word so unseemly,
But all know the proverb, wherein it is said,
That a What is a What, and a Spade is a Spade;
And now I'm provok'd, for a truth I may tell it,
Tho' as red as a fox, yet it smells like a vi'let.
By Jove I'll be judge, if I am not as sweet,
I may say, as a primrose, from head to my feet.
And he, you may swear, who's my husband and lover,
Has kist me, and felt me, and smelt me all over,
And he can say an ill scent does arise,
From my ears, or my armpits, my c——t, or my
    thighs,
Like rotton old Cheshire, low Vervane or Ling,

And altho' I'm goddess, I'll hang in a string.
Your self, Lady Fair, that arose from the sea,
Sure will not presume to be fragrant as me:
The spark that has laid at your feet all his trophies,
Has smelt you sometimes strong as pickl'd anchovies:
But what if he has, where you ranker and older,
You'd be e'en good enough for a smith or a soldier.'
These words put the Goddess of Love in a fire,
And make her look redder than Mars that was by her,
'My beauty,' said Venus, 'obtain'd the Gold Apple.'
'Mine A——s Kiss,' says Juno, 'you shall have a
        couple.
I'd have you to know, Queen of Sluts, I defie you,
And all you can say, or the bully that's by you.
And as for that Tomboy that boasts she can wield,
In quarrels and brangles, her lance and her shield,
That never yet tasted the heavenly blessing,
But always lov'd fighting, much better than kissing:
I know she'd be glad to be ravish'd by force,
By some lusty God, that's as strong as a horse.
But who'd be so forward, unless he was tipsie,
To choose for a miss, such a masculine gipsie?
A termāgant dowdy, a nasty old maid;
Who flights copulation, as if she was spay'd:
Which makes me believe, that under her bodice,
She wants the dear gem, that's the pride of a Goddess.'
Now Pallas, enrag'd at so high a reflection,
Cry'd out, 'I thank Jove, I am made in perfection,
And ev'ry thing have, from a hole to a hair,
Becoming the Goddess of Wisdom and War;
As Paris well knew, when he took a survey,
Of those parts where a Goddess's excellence lay;
Who strok'd it and smil'd, when my legs he had
        parted,
And peep'd till I thought his poor eyes would have
        started.
Then licking his lips, did aver to be true,
I was each way as full well accomplish'd as you.

Indeed, Madam Juno, I'll therefore be plain,
If ever I hear these reflections again:
I vow as a Goddess, and no mortal sinner,
I shall have no patience, but handle your pinner.'
With that the Great Jupiter rose up in hot anger,
And looking on Pallas, was ready to bang her.
'Pox take ye,' says he, 'is your scolding a lecture,
That ought to be preach'd o'er a bowl of good nectar?
To drink we came hither, to sing and be civil;
As gods, to be merry, and not play the devil.
Why, mortals, on earth, that lived crowded in allies,
As laundresses, porters, poor strumpets and bullies;
When got o'er a gallon of belch, or a sneaker
Of punch, could not wrangle, more over their liquor.
And you that are Goddesses, thus to be squabbling,
As if you were bred up to scow'ring and dabbling!
And all for a fig, or a fart, or a feather,
Or some silly thing that's as trivial as either!
For shame, my Fair Goddesses, bridle your passions,
And make not in heaven, such filthy orations
About your bumfiddles; a very fine jest!
When the heavens all know, they but stink at the best.
Tho' ye think you much mend with your washes the
          matter,
And help the ill-scent with your orange flower water;
But when you've done all, 'tis but playing the fool,
And like stifling a T——d, in a cedar close stool:
Besides, Gods of judgment have often confest
That the natural scent without art is the best.'
The Goddesses all, at these sayings, took snuff,
And rose from their seats in a damnable huff:
Their frowns and their blushes, they mingled together,
And went off in a passion, I do not know whither.

'Here's another fine burlesque poem I'll read, if you don't
mind,' continued Frank, 'it's called "Vulcan and Venus."'

VULCAN AND VENUS

Says Vulcan to Venus, 'Pray where have you been?'
'Abroad,' cries the Goddess, 'to see and be seen.'
'I fear,' says the blacksmith, 'you lead an ill life,
Tho' a Goddess, I doubt you're a bitch of a wife.'
'Why, how now,' cries Venus, 'altho' you're my
      spouse,
If you bitch me, you brute, have a care of your brows;
Why sure you don't think, I, the Goddess of Beauty,
By dint of ill language, will prove the more true t'ye;
Be civil, you'd best, or I vow by my placket,
I'll make the god Mars bastinado your jacket!'
'Are you there with your bears!' Smung replies to his
      Hussey.
'Does Mars still refresh your old Furbilo, does he;
I feel by my forehead a coat that is scarlet,
Of all kinds of baits, is the best for a harlot;
For beauty, I find, as 'tis commonly said,
Will nibble like a fish at rag that is red;
But Hussey, tell me any more or your Mars,
And I'll run a hot bar in your Goddesship's arse;
I fear not your threats, there's a fart for your bully,
No whore in the Heavens shall make me her cully!'
'You run a hot bar in my bum,' quoth the dame,
'It's a sign you've a mighty respect for the same;
If your love be so little as to abuse it,
I'll keep it for those who know better to use it;
I'm certain no Goddess that values her honour,
Would bear the indignities you put upon her,
And not from that minute resolve out of spite,
To improve your old horns till they hang in your light.'
'You're an impudent slut,' cries the smung at his
      bellows,
'And I the unhappiest of all marry'd fellows;
I know you have made me a ram, I have seen it,
I catch'd you, you Whore, in the critical minute,
Fast lock'd in the arms of your lecherous God,

Whilst his brawny posteriors went niddity nod;
And you, like a Slut, lay as pleased and contented,
As if every joint of your body consented;
Altho' when you found you were spy'd by your buck,
Then you struggl'd and strove like a pig that is stuck,
And dismounting your God, would have made your
    escape,
But I saw by your actions it could be no rape;
Tho' when you first heard, by my patting-shoe tread,
My approach to your Whoreship's adulterous bed,
I know you'd have flown with your coats and your
    bodice,
And afterwards vow'd 'twas some other lewd Goddess;
But my net was too strong, it prevented your flying,
And so put a stop to your swearing and lying.
Besides, that the Gods might behold what a Slut
Of a Beautiful Queen they amongst them had got,
I call'd 'em about, that their Honours might stand,
And be pimps to your Goddesship's bus'ness in hand,
That in case you the truth shou'd hereafter deny,
I might call the whole Heavens to witness you lie.'
'And what did you get?' cries the amorous dame,
'For the pains that you took, but a Cuckoldy Name;
'Tis true you're confirmed you've a Whore for your
    wife,
Pray is that any comfort or ease to your life;
And have made it appear to the Gods as a jest,
That your wife's reputation is none of the best;
Does that make your labour more easy or sweet,
Or give you more gust to your drink or your meat?
'Tis true, you are fam'd for the net you have made,
Pray what did you catch in't but horns for your head;
You know that your rival don't value a trap,
Or a net, any more than a child or a clap;
A soldier is never asham'd of his vices,
But rather is proud of a Goddess's kisses;
And thinks it adds more to a hero's renown,
To subdue a fair lady than conquer a town;

Your spite must be therefore intended alone,
Against me, and that my little faults might be known;
Since 'tis as it is, I am very well pleas'd,
Your head shall be loaded, my tail shall be eas'd;
For since you have publish'd my shame and disgrace,
And have made me a jest to the heavenly race;
I'll be impudent now, and whenever I meet,
My dear favourite Mars, tho' it be in the street;
If a bulk be but near, I will never more dally,
He shall, if it pleases him, ay marry shall he;
Thus all you shall get by your open detection,
Of one silly error in female affection,
Is a wife that will cuckold you worse out of spite,
Now she's catch'd, than before she e're did for delight;
To punish my head and heart, that very vice,
Which I us'd but in private whilst honour was nice;
I'll publickly now practice over and o'er,
Till thou'rt fain'd for a Cuckold and I for a Whore.'
Cries Vulcan, 'Could ever man think that a Goddess,
Admir'd for her charms by such numbers of noddies,
Should ever be curst with so rampant a tail,
That will wallow more love-sap, that I can do ale;
A pox on your rump, for I plainly see 'tis
As salt as your parents, Oceanus and Tethys,
But had I first known you had sprung from salt water,
The Devil for me, should have marry'd the daughter;
Besides, you are grown both so lustful and bold,
And for all your sweet looks, have a Billingsgate
      tongue,
That is fifty times worse than a fisherman's hung.
If these be the plagues of a beautiful wife,
O ease me, Great Jove, of so cursed a life;
If La Pies divine, who inhabit the Heavens,
Will Whore on like morals, at sixes and sevens;
Rave, rattle, and taunt at their horrify'd spouses,
And ramble abitching thro' all the twelve houses;
For all your fine features I'll e'en give you over,
The charms of a Whore are but plagues to a lover.

Get you gone and be pox'd, to your old bully Mars,
Let a God be a slave to your Goddesship's A——s;
Whilst I'm contempt of your infamous rump,
On my anvil will knock, with a thump, a thump-
        thump!'

The second day after Frank had read these curious old bits to
his parents and sister, they were all delighted by the arrival of
young Harry Mortimer to spend a day with his old
school-mate.

To judge by appearances Mr Etheridge had every cause for
the curious desires he had confessed to, two days before.
Harry was a really handsome youth of seventeen, with golden
coloured hair, the bloom of the peach on his cheeks, and most
lovable pair of deep blue eyes which seemed full of the humid
fire of love. He had also a finely developed form, which his
close-fitting garments set off to the best advantage, and,
above all, what had the most charm for the eyes of his friends
as they so heartily welcomed him to their house was the evidently precocity of his organs of love, which in their quiescent
state showed a most prominent lump in house trousers.

Mrs Etheridge: 'Why Harry, what a fine fellow you have
grown since I saw you a year ago. No doubt you are too
bashful to kiss Ethel now, but you will surely embrace an old
friend like me, who used to nurse you in my arms as a baby,'
giving him such an amorous hug and smack upon his cheeks
that the young fellow blushed up to his eyes.

After luncheon Frank took Harry for a walk, and asking
him if he would like to look at their horses, they bent their
steps to the stables where the groom Thomas, a fine
handsome young fellow of about twenty, was polishing the
coats of his charges, at the same time as he emitted that
curious hissing which all stablemen so mysteriously
accustom themselves to when busy over their work. He did
not see the two young gentlemen till they had been watching
his operations for a few seconds, but as soon as he did so,
respectfully touched his cap and asked them to look at his
horses.

Walking into the stable, Thomas, cap in hand, respectfully pointed out all the perfections of his pets and the neatness of all the appointments. Then he conducted them into the harness room, which was at the top of a short flight of stairs.

Thomas was about to close an interior door, which half open gave a view into his own private quarters, when, a sudden idea striking him, Frank said, 'You don't mind, Thomas, if we take a peep into your sanctum – unless you have got a young lady you would rather we did not see. I only want to let Mr Mortimer see how cosy your room is, besides, you know, I have often had a sly smoke with you there on wet days when I was home for the holidays before, and I know you have always got some nice clean glasses in your cupboard, if not anything better than water to offer us. But I have taken care of that and brought a good flask of finest brandy. I got the housekeeper to give me some of papa's real *vieux cognac*. It's ever so old and goes down like milk. Just the thing, Thomas, to keep you up to your work when you have a nice girl. But I forgot you never do anything of the sort, eh! How about little Lucy, the under-housemaid, who I hear had to go home with a big belly not long ago?'

'Lord, sir!' said Thomas, quite enjoying Frank's joke, 'that'll be another of old Stroker's kids when its born. He did it when she went up to be taught her confirmation lesson. I'm told he confirmed seven girls in fucking, this examination. He's a regular ram of a parson, and will soon be the father of all the young'uns in the parish. I wonder Master let Miss Ethel go to him at all. I always suspected the old fellow after the way he treated me.'

They entered the snug little bedroom, where everything was as clean as a new pin, and seated themselves on the only two chairs that were there, whilst the groom brought out the glasses and fetched a jug of bright sweet spring water from the pump outside.

Frank, mixing a rather stiffish drop, said, 'Now, Thomas, drink the Rev Mr Stroker's health, and then tell us all about his tricks with you.'

Himself and Harry also took a little of the brandy. And Thomas, pressed to begin, cleared his throat and commenced:

'Well, Mr Frank and Mr Mortimer, I don't mind letting you into the secret, but the fact is every time I think of the old rascal's indecency it makes my cock stand, but you must not tell a soul what I now tell you.'

'All right, go on, old fellow, just a drop more brandy to encourage your bashfulness, eh!' laughed Frank.

Thomas, wiping his mouth after a good swig at the brandy and water: 'Well, sirs, that righteous old sinner, as an Irishman would say, began by asking me questions about who made me. If I knew there was a God and a Devil. Then about the world and the flesh, and so on, a lot of rubbish out of the church prayerbook. "You know, Thomas, my boy," he said, "that the 'flesh' means having do to with girls and other dirty indecent things which come into the heads of rude boys. Now tell me if you ever did anything of that kind with other boys or girls?"

'This was rather a poser for me. I don't like to tell a downright lie and knew I had been a party to one or two little games of that sort, such as we used to do in the hayfield, throwing the girls down, turning up their clothes, and showing them our cocks, which no doubt the old rascal knew. I could feel my face was turning quite red with confusion. "Ha, I see what it is, Thomas! I must thoroughly examine you and tell by the look of your penis" (that is the word I think he used, but you know he meant my cock), as he ordered me to unbutton and show him my privates, and he would soon tell if I had been up to any of the Devil's wickedness.

'As soon as I was exposed to him he told me to draw the skin of my cock back, which I did.

'"Do it again, my boy, there now, again – two of three times mind."

'Then I expect he saw slight signs of a rise, saying, "Do it quicker – quicker, boy" till I had the horn quite stiff.

'"My gracious! You're finely grown for your age, Thomas. Now did you never show that to a gal?"

'"Well, sir," I said, rather shamefaced at what he was making me do, "I did once, but only once, sir, and Polly Jones felt it with her hand, and let me feel what her cock was like, too."

'"Fine goings on in my parish, 'pon my word, Thomas, but what sort of thing had she got? Because you know gals have nothing like this," he said, taking hold of my standing prick.

'"She'd – she'd only a little crack, sir," I replied. "Pray let me go now, sir, I don't like it." He was regularly frigging me.

'"Silly boy, here's a half-crown to keep quiet, if you let me handle it a bit, and you shall have another every time you come to me," he said, giving me the money, and soon frigged me to a spend and then let me go. I didn't think much harm in it, and was very glad to get the parson's half-crowns, so went twice a week for examination. He wasn't satisfied with just frigging me, but sometimes went down on his knees and sucked my cock till I spent in his mouth, which I liked better, but when he wanted me to do the same for him, and even offered me a sovereign, I wouldn't do it, only let him rub his great cock against my belly and balls, and then he would spend, holding the head of my prick against his own and so drawing his own foreskin over it. Then I had the sovereign, never to open my lips about it, and at last was confirmed.'

Frank now gave Thomas a drop more brandy and asked him if he would like to be mesmerized, adding, 'If you are game to let me, you will then have to answer truthfully any questions I ask and do everything I tell you.'

Thomas: 'Now, Mr Frank, you are trying to get at me – as if I would believe that, I ain't afraid. You may try.'

Frank: 'Then look me steadily in the face, and let me hold you by your two thumbs.'

Thomas: 'All right, sir, but I be sure you can't make me do as you say.'

For a little while he resisted the effects of Frank's mesmeric art, but in less than five minutes his eyes had a quite vacant look, and in obedience to his young master he seated himself on the side of the bed.

'Now, Harry, let me do you as well, as I have an idea I want to carry out.'

'You may take hold of my thumbs as you did with Thomas, but I defy you to mesmerize me,' said Harry, laughing.

'That's too bad,' replied Frank with a smile, 'but there's no harm in trying what I can do, old fellow, eh?'

It was a hard task to fix the gaze of his youthful companion, but by patience and perseverence Frank succeeded at last in putting him also into a perfect state of mesmeric sleep.

'Now, my fine fellows, I shall be well rewarded for my trouble before I bring you round again, and it's my turn before I fetch Papa on the scene, I think.'

He stripped himself, and ordered his two subjects to do the same, put a small box of cold cream under the pillow of the bed so as to be at hand, then contemplated and handled the young groom and his friend.

Thomas was furnished with a lovely tosser, which swelled rapidly under his touches as he uncovered the ruby head and gently pulled the foreskin backward and forward.

'Now, Thomas, keep yourself stiff by gentle frigging, but mind not to spend till I order you,' he said; then he turned to the beautiful Harry Mortimer, who came to his side as soon as ordered. He was indeed an Adonis – splendidly shaped in every limb, delightfully plump and firm white flesh, rosy cheeks, sparkling blue eyes – but Frank was so engrossed with his jewel of a prick, which was a perfect gem of the first water, nearly eight inches long when erect, as white and hard as ivory, yet of velvety softness to the touch, and set in a bed of soft, curly, golden-brown hair, which ornamented the roots and shaded the full bag of tricks in their receptacle below.

How Frank handled, caressed, and kissed this treasure of

love, as he ejaculated, 'Oh, Papa, oh Mamma, what a thrill the sight of this will give you both. But I must enjoy it first!'

Placing himself on the bed, sitting up with his back supported by a pillow, he ordered Thomas to straddle his lap. Taking up the box of cream, he first anointed the head of his own impatient priapus, then did the same to Thomas' fundament, working his two fingers well in it, which made the groom's prick throb and stiffen enormously. Then Frank adjusted his tool to the wrinkled orifice; in obedience to his mysterious influence Thomas slowly impaled himself upon it, till his buttocks embraced its whole length and Frank had his man's cock deliciously chafing and rubbing between their naked bellies at every movement. Passing his hands under Thomas' armpits, Harry was made to come forwards behind the groom and present his glorious prick over the left shoulder so that Frank could take that lovely ruby head in his mouth, whilst his hands drew back the foreskin and tickled and played with its appendages, the mere touch of which filled Frank with maddening lust.

Never had he experienced such ecstasy and erotic fury as this conjuction with his groom and friend now caused him to feel, he thrilled from head to toe with voluptuous excitement as his spendings seemed to shoot from him again and again, with a very few seconds between each emission, whilst Harry on his part deluged his mouth and lips with the balmy juice of his virginity and Thomas also flooded his belly with convulsive jets of spunk, all of them being so young and vigorous they seemed almost inexhaustible.

At last Frank began to feel it was too much and sank back, overcome by such an acme of enjoyment, as his prick dropped gradually out of the groom's fundus.

Presently recovering himself a little, he took a sip of neat brandy, hastily dressed himself, and willing his subjects to lie quietly on the bed till he came back, he ran with bated breath, and flushed as he was with delight, to call his father and mother to the scene.

They all came back together after the lapse of a few

163

minutes. Papa and Mamma, on entering the little bedroom over the stable, were struck at once by the entrancing sight which met their eyes, of these two beautiful young fellows lying naked on the bed; but in a minute or two both of them threw off all their clothing, in order to thoroughly avail themselves of the treat provided by their dutiful son.

Frank, by his influence, now willed Harry to kneel up on the bed on his hands and knees, whilst Thomas was to lie flat on his back.

Mr Etheridge, who had brought a fine dildo with him, now put cold cream on it and also on Harry's bum-hole, then inserting the instrument slowly it gradually won its way in, and he watched its effects with delight as young Mortimer's cock began to stand again in all its previous glory. He mounted on the couch behind him, and withdrawing the dildo, put his own rampant prick in its place, having first lubricated it with cold cream, then clasping his arms around the dear youth, he frigged that fine prick, exactly as Frank had seen the professor do with the boy at college.

Mrs Etheridge waited a few moments watching her spouse's operation till her blood was so fired with amorous excitement that she at once seized upon Thomas' cock, which was lying rather limp between his fine thighs, then forcing his legs a little further apart, she gamahuched him and licked his splendid balls till he was as stiff as ever; then mounting upon her man she slowly impaled herself upon his luscious battering ram as she lowered her body till her lips met his in a fiery voluptuousness, to which, under Frank's mysterious influence, the groom responded with all the ardour of his nature.

For a few moments Mrs Etheridge continued to kiss and thrust her tongue into Thomas' mouth, whilst she kept her buttocks steady and revelled in the sense of possession which that fine prick afforded her, as her cunt felt thoroughly gorged by the delicious morsel.

Frank, who had intended to enjoy the scene as a passive spectator, was again fired by the sight of such a voluptuous

164

group, his prick beginning to stiffen again, notwithstanding his previous exhaustion, so mounting on the bed he faced his Papa, and letting down his trousers presented his half erect cock to Harry Mortimer's lips, as he willed him to take it in his mouth and suck it lusciously. The youth's lips opened mechanically, the very first touch of them sending a thrill of pleasure through Frank's frame so that he stiffened up immediately, and fucked the boy's mouth gently, so as not to come again too soon.

Mr and Mrs Etheridge both spent quickly, being each of them so excited by the idea of what they were doing, but keeping their places they all went on without stopping, Papa frigging his dear boy Harry, and making his prick spend copiously, receiving the love juice in his hand and rubbing it deliciously over the hills and shaft of the cock he was caressing.

They kept it up deliberately and slowly for some time, so as to enjoy the two fine young fellows to the utmost, then all come together with screams and cries of ecstacy – Frank seeming to control the whole party by his mesmeric influence in such a way that their very souls vibrated in accordance with his wishes, the enjoyment of father, mother, and son being simply inexpressible.

'Ah, Frank, my dear boy,' sighed Mr Etheridge, 'you have afforded us a heavenly treat, but it must now come to an end or we may some of us actually expire under such excessive emotions.'

After dressing and willing the two subjects also to assume their clothes, Papa and Mamma went away. Frank recalled Thomas and Harry to consciousness and bantered them about the games he had made them go through at his command. 'Would you believe it? You did anything I ordered – sucking each other's pricks, and frigging each other, and doing exactly what I liked to order.'

Neither of them would believe it, saying they had only been off for a very short time and that he had tumbled the bed to make believe what he said of them was true. At the same time both admitted having had very confused though pleasing dreams.

A few days after what has just been related, Harry Mortimer paid them another visit, which the family council had resolved should be a regular 'mesmeric séance.'

Besides their young friend they had invited the rector of the parish, Dr Stroker, and his two nieces, Blanche and Ada Manners, very pretty brunettes of sixteen and seventeen.

The day passed delightfully on the grounds where they played croquet, or retired to the summer house for refreshment.

During the course of the afternoon Mamma and the parson took a walk by themselves. Mrs Etheridge, with assumed unconsciousness, pointing out the beauties of the flowers, or calling his attention to the occasional glimpses of the sea, which they obtained through openings of the landscape, till they neared a rustic seat, where she declared she was so very fatigued she must rest awhile if the Doctor did not object.

Seating herself with a slight sigh of relief, she remarked, 'How tiring the game of croquet always seemed,' adding, 'do you not think it is quite absurd for us old people to join with the young ones in such games?'

'My dear Madame,' replied the Doctor, 'we are always children as long as we live. We enjoy the games of youth with zest, even if we have not the same powers, and it is the same with love, which so enthralls us that I verily believe the older we get the more enthusiastic we become in its pursuit. Now confess, my dear Mrs Etheridge, is it not so with you?'

'Fie, Doctor, pray don't take advantage of our secluded position to press that hopeless, wicked suit of yours. Besides, sir,' she added with a laugh, 'this is, you know, Saturday afternoon, and such thoughts can only be prompted by the devil to drive out of your mind all your ideas for tomorrow's sermon.'

The parson now ventured to put his arm round the voluptuous waist, as he drew closer still to his lovely companion, saying, 'No fear of that, my dear Madame. Can you guess what my test is to be tomorrow?'

'How could I, you silly man?' said Mrs Etheridge with a very encouraging smile. 'Is it anything out of the common?'

'Well, hem – I think it so, Madame, and one that will bring your sins of omission to your conscience,' answered he.

'Don't keep me in suspense, but tell me at once, you foolish fellow, you know I can't guess.'

'Can't guess – can't guess even! How you do dissimulate, Mrs Etheridge, when I know you're always thinking of it, my dear lady. Well then, it's – it's prick – no, I mean the first commandment – you know what this is surely, look at this fine specimen of the Creator's work, and say if you can despise his command, "to be fruitful and multiply, and replenish the earth,"' he said, placing in her hand his great big standing priapus which he had let out of his trousers.

The touch was electric, a shiver of desire ran through her whole frame, as her fingers seemed to grasp the lovely jewel without knowing what she was about; her eyes closed and she sank back apparently shocked and helpless on the seat.

'Dear lady,' the Doctor went on, 'the Devil can never prevent me preaching from that text. I could speak extempore upon it for hours, it was the very first command both to Adam and also to Noah when he came out of the ark. Dear Mrs Etheridge, let me touch that divine cunt of yours. I can't make out what your husband has been about since the charming Ethel was born that you have had no more children, you surely have not obeyed that command-ment!'

His hands were already under her dress, feeling those splendid thighs, and gradually working their way up to the seat of bliss.

Mrs Etheridge's whole form heaved with emotion, he could feel her quiver under his touches, and mistook it for the modesty of her nature rebelling at the libidinous thoughts which his rude proceeding aroused within her, whereas, in reality, it arose from the unbounded lubricity of

167

her nature, now fired by the intensity of her desires.

The Reverend Dr Stroker was no timid gallant; he proceeded with rapidity from one liberty to another, throwing the lady into still greater confusion. Pressing his lips to hers, he seemed ready to devour her with his fiery kisses, while Mrs Etheridge also was utterly bereft of power to resist his advances, so pulling up her clothes he forced his legs between her yielding thighs, and soon brought the nose of Mr Peaslin to the mark. As it just touched the lips of that seraphic cunt the effect was irresistible on the slightly struggling lady, who suddenly opened her legs as widely as possible to meet his charge, and throwing her arms around his neck, returned his kisses with equal ardour as she sighed, 'Oh, I am undone, give it me now, dear Doctor, but oh! oh!! oh!!! how shall we take the Holy Communion tomorrow?' as he thrust so vigorously that she was almost beside herself with delight.

'This is the real communion, tomorrow's ceremony is only a farce. Do you think that anyone is ever really fit according to the rubric? Away with such silly nonsense, there is nothing in heaven or earth to compare with the delights of coition!' And his movements went on, each stroke of that fine cock filling her vagina to repletion, and arousing every muscle and membrane of her body to the acme of felicity.

At last both spent together, and they were lying in the state of lethargic enjoyment when the sound of laughter at a distance soon roused them to a sense of their exposed position, and they had barely time to set things straight before Mr Etheridge, Frank, Harry, and the three girls came upon the scene.

No particular remarks were made at the time, but significant glances from Mrs Etheridge informed her husband and children of the pleasure she had just tasted.

They returned to the house for dinner, and afterwards having adjourned to the drawing room, Mrs Etheridge ordered the servants to have coffee and refreshments ready in the ante-room, but upon no account to disturb their party, as the Doctor was going to give a scientific lecture.

As soon as the servants were gone the parson expressed his surprise at Mrs Etheridge's announcement, being, as he said, utterly unprepared to give lectures at a minute's warning. To which the hostess replied with a slightly ironical tone in her voice. 'But, Doctor, you told me this afternoon you could lecture upon and illustrate the first commandment at any time. However, if you do not feel equal to lecturing for our amusement, my Frank shall show some of his mesmeric tricks which he acquired in Germany, and you shall be his first subject.'

'Not the slightest objection in the world to that, if it will amuse you, my dear Mrs Etheridge,' replied the rector, 'but don't tell me afterwards that I have been confessing to all sorts of scandalous things, because I know these mesmeric lectures can make their subjects say anything.'

During this dialogue Frank had, unobserved by the others, quietly put Miss Blanche into a state of unconsciousness, then turning to Harry told him that if he would submit to be again operated upon, he could make him and the Doctor's niece dance and sing to his orders to amuse the company.

Harry Mortimer was too good-natured to refuse, and after him Frank also put the parson and Ada Manners into the same state, then as he looked around upon his parents and sisters he asked them, with a look of triumph, what the programme was to be.

Ethel: 'You left me out of the little party over the stable the other afternoon, so now it is my turn to be considered.'

Papa: 'By all means, my darling, only say what you wish for.'

Ethel: 'Then we will all strip, and as I wish particularly to feel that great and reverend prick, I will kneel on the couch and have the Doctor dog fashion, so we can see all what is going on. First make the two girls frig each other, then they shall be made to do the same to Harry and Frank, who will afterwards take their virginities, whilst you and Mamma will be delighted to gamahuche and help the operation, and

169

after that we will be guided by our fancies.'

This pleased everyone. The subjects were made to strip off everything except the ladies' boots and stockings, presenting a most luscious sight to the free-loving family. Then to make up a tableau Frank willed that the Doctor, naked as he was, should take and seat his two nieces on his knees, and under his influence each of the two sisters at once extended a hand to grasp his glorious prick, which at the same time rose in all its pride of strength, so that their delicate hands, one above the other on its shaft, still left the purple head towering above the uppermost by tow or three inches at least.

Harry also took his place by the side of Ada, who caressed his stiffened cock with her disengaged hand, whilst Blanche did the same to Frank, who had stripped and stood by her side to complete the group.

Beautiful as was this scene, Ethel lost very little time before she placed herself on the couch on all fours, and as Frank ordered his subjects, the two nieces fairly dragged their uncle by his prick, till they got him up behind Ethel, and planted the head of his fiery steed just within the lips of her longing cunt.

Mr and Mrs Etheridge now produced their birch rods, and began to stimulate the parson with a shower of stinging cuts, the tips of the birch often also touching up Ethel's bum or thighs and adding very materially to her erotic enjoyment, as the Doctor fucked in a perfect fury of lust under the effects of the birching, which fairly scored his firm, hard flesh, breaking the skin and drawing little drops of blood.

Meanwhile Frank had conducted Harry Mortimer and the rector's nieces to another part of the room, and willed the two girls to frig each other. They were perfectly amenable to his every wish, Blanche stretching herself at full length on a fine rug made of the skin of wild cats (which are said to have such exciting effects on those who recline upon them).

Ada was made to reverse herself upon her elder sister,

and each opening their legs with the utmost freedom, frigged and gamahuched each other's cunts in such a luscious manner as left little doubt in Frank's mind that the two young girls had often before had rehearsals of the same game in private.

The mesmerizer and his young friend knelt down also on the rug on either side of the tribades, and facing each other, embraced with the most apparent ardour across the bodies of the writhing and excitable girls. Each of them put an arm round the other's neck, their lips meeting in the most wanton manner possible as they sucked each other's tongues, whilst their disengaged hands were applied to their respective pricks, till the spending moment came upon the group simultaneously – the two girls almost fainting from excess of pleasure as they emitted their virgin love juice, whilst the young fellows above them also spent as they held the noses of their pricks together, letting the overflow of sperm sprinkle all over Blanche and Ada below.

The other group had had an equally ecstatic finish, Ethel pushing back her bottom upon the parson's prick at the critical moment with all the energy of her maddening lust, and receiving within the inmost recess of her insatiable womb a perfect torrent of bliss, making her fairly scream with delight as she sank down on the couch from the voluptuous exhaustion of the moment, the folds of her cunt tightening and throbbing upon his delighted prick in such a way that it retained its stiffness, and soon recommenced another thrilling course with Ethel lying flat under him face downwards. It was a delicious situation – she held him so tightly, although his prick did not go so far in, that he screamed out, 'Holy Moses, what a fuck! Her cunt's as tight as a boy's arsehole!' as he clung to her and ground his teeth in the height of his excitement.

Mr Etheridge was behind him now, and using some cold cream on the Doctor's rough-looking, brown, wrinkled bottom-hole, presented his cock to the mark, and clinging tightly round his waist soon gained admission by the reverend back door. How tight and warm it was to his excited priapus, which answered by a thrust to every heave of the parson's bottom as he fucked the dear girl beneath him.

Mamma also, not to be left out of the game, mounted on the long couch, and lying on her back in front of her daughter, opened her thighs so as to embrace Ethel's face and present her longing cunt for her to suck. Then reclining her head and shoulders on a large cushion, she called for Frank and Harry to leave the two girls, and come on either side of her so that they could both present the heads of their pricks to her lips, whilst she handled their balls and frigged them till they shot into her mouth a double flow of the nectar of love which she so loved to drain to the very last drop.

Papa revelled in his rear attack as his hand fondled with delight the Doctor's prick and balls at every withdrawal from Ethel's cunt, the lips of which he could also feel as they tenaciously clung round the shaft of that fine instrument, which was giving such pleasure at every thrust.

At this juncture Frank willed the parson to awake from the mesmeric trance. His eyes resumed their wanton intelligence, and as he at once realised the situation, his usual sanctified exclamation of horror, 'How awful, what have they been doing to me!' Then, 'Oh, it must be a dream of my old college days, by Jove, how we fucked and buggered at Oxford!'

'That's right, Doctor,' laughed Frank, 'now you are beginning to fairly comprehend how we are punishing you for taking advantage of Mamma this afternoon, only it's pleasure instead of pain, old boy. But we thought anyone with such a glorious prick as yours ought not to be too hardly treated.'

The spasm of pleasure prevented further speech at the moment, fairly carrying away the whole group by the intensity of the sensations which such erratic voluptuousness could not fail to produce upon natures which, after all, were only sustained by the ordinary powers of humanity, in fact it was too exhaustive to allow of further indulgence in

172

venery upon the present occasion. But after recovering a little, the Doctor, who now thoroughly relished the idea, proposed that Harry, Blanche, and Ada should be still kept in their entranced state to afford them amusement, as he said it would be a fine treat to make them tell all the little games they had been up to.

The three subjects were not allowed to dress, but all the others now resumed their clothes, then the parson proceeded to catechise them.

Q. – Blanche, did you ever hear how babies are made?

A. – A girl at school told me the men shove their cocks into the girls, and shoot their spunk into them, which makes the babies.

Q. – Do the girls like to have that done to them?

A. – Yes, it's awfully funny and nice, makes our cunts what they call spend with pleasure.

Q. – Have you ever felt anything of it yourself? Do the girls play at fathers and mothers at school?

A. – Nearly every night we used to change bedfellows for the purpose of having a fresh bit of cock, as we used to call their fingers.

Q. – Go on, tell us all about it.

A. – Some of the girls used a candle or the finger of a glove stuffed out to make a little prick, a well greased carrot was fine I can tell you. Once they nearly drove me mad with delight by fucking me with a carrot, whilst another girl used a tallow candle in my bumhole till nothing but the wick was left. But I felt awfully bad next day, and you can fancy I passed tallow when I went to the closet.

Q. – Well, and how did Ada get on?

A. – She did not sleep in our room, she was with the French governess.

Q. – Now, Ada, you must tell us all you know.

A. – The French governness was so hairy and rude, she began by tickling my fanny till I didn't know what I was doing, then she laid me back on the bed, and forced her face between my thighs, and sucked my cunny.

Q. – Well, go on, out with everything.

A. – After a while she would lay over me, and make me kiss her great hairy slit. Oh, you should have seen what a lot of hair she had on her belly, as black as jet right up to her navel. And then she used to wriggle about, and wet all my lips and face, which she called spending. A favourite game of hers was to make me frig her by forcing as much as I could of one of my titties into her cunt, which seemed to drive her almost wild; she would kiss my legs, feet, and any part she could reach in a frantic way whilst I was doing it.

Q. – Did she never do the same thing to you?

A. – Yes, it was awfully fine to feel her titty and nipple rubbing just inside the lips of my little cunny, I believe she made me spend – at least, I fainted and found myself all wet afterwards.

Q. – What other rude games have you been up to, by yourself or with your sister?

A. – When we were home for the holidays we used to frig each other with our fingers or titties, the latter was quite a new idea to Blanche. We used to watch our mother and father doing it to each other on Sunday afternoons. They would always go upstairs after lunch 'to have a rest' but we knew what they were really up to. We used to watch them through the key-hole. Mama would pretend she was a horse and Papa would ride her naked around the room, smacking her great big bottom cheeks until they were all red and wobbly while he shouted 'Tally-ho!'

Q. – Now, Harry, when did you first touch a girl's thing?

A. – I suppose I was about fourteen when that happened. My aunt Clara, a very beautiful young widow of twenty-three, who had just lost my uncle (her husband) in the terrible Clayton Tunnel accident, and I may here add that what hurt her sensitive feelings almost more than his loss was the fact the the gay young fellow had taken a girl on the sly with him to Brighton for the day, and you know it was on the return journey that the collision occurred. Well, her grief and thoughts of his conduct, she said, made her so nervous and low spirited that she begged my Mamma to allow little Harry, as she called me, to go and stay with her for a time as companion. Every morning we would come into my bedroom to awaken me with a loving kiss, pulling off the bed-clothes, and playing me all sorts of tricks to make me get up. On one occasion, feeling unusually tired, I begged she would let me lay only a few minutes longer, as I drew her beautiful face down to my lips and smothered her with kisses. I was almost uncovered at the moment, it was a bright May morning, and the glorious sun was flooding the apartment with his beams of light and warmth. 'My darling boy,' she said softly, 'I have a slight headache, and will rest on the bed by your side a little while,' throwing her arms around me, and nestling her soft cheeks against mine. I soon felt her hands wandering over every part of my body, but it was so nice that when I felt her touch my naked thigh, I felt a curious kind of alloverishness, and my little prick stood as stiff as a poker. At last she touched even that. My eyes were apparently closed, pretending to be in a doze, but I could see the blush that came into her cheeks, and felt her give a kind of shudder all over. She caressed my little cocky for a moment or two, which gave me a kind of longing for her to go on. I could see she was greatly agitated, but my own sense of pleasure prevented me thinking much about that. My heart seemed to go out to her in a gush of love, as I suddenly opened my eyes, and throwing my arms around her neck once more, kissed her again and again.

How her eyes sparkled, and she seemed to blush deeper than ever, but her soft hand never let go of the little treasure she had secured.

'Harry, my dear boy, is your little affair often like this? It is quite unnaturally hard,' she asked me in a low, husky kind of whisper. 'Perhaps you are ill, my dear, let me see,' saying which she threw back the bed-clothes, and examined my privates, handling my stiff pintle very tenderly, as if she really thought there might be something the matter with me, and finished by kissing my cock and taking the poor thing in her mouth as she said it must be quite painful to bear. You may guess that the only effect of her endearments was to make my affair swell up bigger than I had ever known it, as well as putting me in a kind of flutter all over, in fact I can't describe how she made me feel.

The next night I had been asleep about a couple of hours when I was suddenly awakened by someone bringing a light into my room; it was Auntie Clara in her nightdress. 'Harry,' she said, 'I feel so nervous, pray do come and sleep with me, I don't like to ask the servants, and you can slip back into your room in the morning.'

I was too pleased to say no, and soon found myself in her bed nestling close to her, with my face between her soft bubbies. She at once asked me if my affair was stiff, and seemed astonished to find it again hard when she caressed it, as I told her it had been quite limp all day.

She kissed me again and again, telling me it proved I was getting to be a man. 'But, Harry darling, you must never say a word about it. Would you like to be my little husband and always sleep with me?'

'Oh, Auntie, that would be delightful, would you marry me if I was a man?' I asked in reply.

'Yes, darling, and I will wait till you grow up, if you promise now to be my husband, and keep secret everything between us.'

How we played together after I gave her my solemn promise. She let me feel her all over, got out of bed, lighted three or four candles, and stripped herself quite naked for me to see what she was like. She made me kiss her lovely cunt, all covered and shaded by dark chestnut hair, as it was, and assured me I should soon also have hair round the roots of my cock, then she shocked me how to be a husband to her, and made me work my little cock in her till she almost drowned it in her spendings.

So you see I have been engaged to be married ever since then, and every time we have a chance Aunt Clara accords me all the rights of a husband. She says we have only to wait a year or two now, as she has a handsome income, enough for both if my parents object.

This was the end of the séance, the subjects were all put in order and restored to consciousness, and the Doctor quietly whispered to Mr and Mrs Etheridge that he should like to bring his two nieces after the Sunday evening service, to be mesmerized again and have their maidenheads taken, it would be such a treat to see it done.

It is not necessary to weary the reader by full details of how Frank and Harry did this for them, to complete the satisfaction of their reverend uncle, who again enjoyed the delights of being sandwiched between his host and hostess, and helped them to realise every erotic imagination of their hearts.

By way of conclusion it will perhaps be interesting to relate the experiences of a young lady (none other than Minette) who paid a visit to this charming family in later days.

The account is taken from a letter sent to a gentleman friend, to whom she was much attached at the time.

One day we were all taken into what I imagined to be the drawing room, but afterwards ascertained it was a place strictly confined to the private use of the family and that but one confidential servant was ever allowed to enter it, for the purpose of cleaning, dusting, and keeping it in order. The walls were hung with pictures of the most exciting character, and in the centre of the room was a huge bed, covered with crimson velvet and stuffed with down, but without any of the ordinary bed-clothing, instead there were a quantity of cushions variously shaped and also covered with velvet. Some of these were fitted with concealed dildoes, so that when pressed between the thighs the most delightful frigging could be produced. Some were fitted with artificial cunts for the use of gentlemen, if they felt so inclined. There were flogging machines of every description, and various articles of furniture for supporting the body in peculiar positions which might be required while being fucked, sucked, or buggered.

The door was no sooner closed than I was seized by Frank and his mother and tumbled on the bed, where they rummaged every part of my body, bottom-hole, cunt, and bubbies, and at last forced one of the dildo-cushions between my thighs and compelled me to frig myself upon it, while they pulled up my clothes and slapped my poor arse for some minutes without mercy, laughing and enjoying my screams as my tender rump plunged up and down in exquisite pain.

Ethel was helping them by sitting on my shoulders so that I was quite powerless, but when they presently desisted from that cruel slapping and I felt tongue, finger, or prick alternately forced up my bottom, it was delicious – the heat of the previous infliction making me feel so lecherous that the spunk actually spurted from my quim as I wriggled myself up and down on the dildo.

Ethel I found also (as soon as the paroxysm of spending had allayed my feelings a little, and I was allowed to look around) was sucking her father's prick, whilst he was frigging her.

Next, the servant Maud entered the room and was immediately stripped to the skin and bound to a flogging machine, where they birched her deliciously (at least it looked so to me, although she screamed and writhed about in pain, and begged for mercy as the tears streamed down her face), till she was on the verge of spending. She was then left to suffer the agonies of unsatisfied desire, while we enacted all the most lascivious things we could think of in her sight.

I took Mr Etheridge's prick and frigged it between my bubbies, whilst he sucked the prick of his son.

We then tickled the girl's inflamed cunt with stinging nettles, which increased her excitment till she seemed mad with erotic delirium, and Mr Etheridge, to my horror, proposed that we should injure her as a finish to our orgy for that evening.

Mr Etheridge drove his tremendously inflamed prick into her bottom-hole, the position in which she was suspended making the operation awfully painful. Frank fucked the poor girl in the cunt. Mrs Etheridge and Ethel, with savage pleasure, each sucked and bit the victim's nipples, causing her to writhe and scream in ecstasy. The two fuckers were at the same time frigging mother and daughter, whilst they passed the sensation on to me by also manipuluting my cunt and bottom.

Before my visit terminated there was another orgy, in which Harry Mortimer introduced his Aunt Clara to this amiable family circle. Mesmerism was now quite unnecessary, Harry being as willing a votary to the worship of Priapus as could possibly be desired by his erotic friends.

The principal scene of the evening was a group in which the beautiful Aunt Clara rode a St George upon Mr Etheridge, had Harry in her bottom-hole, Frank's prick in her mouth, her two hands frigging Mrs Etheridge and Ethel as they stood by the side of the couch, whilst your *chère amie*, not to be let out of the game, was behind Harry, my left hand passed round his loins, caressing his fine prick and balls as it worked in and out of her beautiful brown bumhole, whilst my right forefinger postilioned him behind.

You must imagine the excitement of this group so voluptuously arranged; it requires to be engaged in such a scene to fully appreciate all its heavenly delights – description is simply impossible!

MORE EROTIC CLASSICS FROM CARROLL & GRAF

☐ Anonymous/SATANIC VENUS		$4.50
☐ Anonymous/SECRET LIVES		$3.95
☐ Anonymous/SENSUAL SECRETS		$4.50
☐ Anonymous/SWEET TALES		$4.50
☐ Anonymous/THREE TIMES A WOMAN		$3.95
☐ Anonymous/VENUS DISPOSES		$3.95
☐ Anonymous/VENUS UNBOUND		$3.95
☐ Anonymous/THE WANTONS		$3.95
☐ Anonymous/WAYWARD VENUS		$4.50
☐ Anonymous/A WOMAN OF PLEASURE		$3.95
☐ Anonymous/WHITE THIGHS		$4.50
☐ Cleland, John/FANNY HILL		$4.95
☐ Perez, Faustino/LA LOLITA		$3.95
☐ Thornton, Louise, *et al.*/TOUCHING FIRE		$9.95
☐ van Heller, Marcus/THE LOINS OF AMON		$3.95
☐ van Heller, Marcus/ROMAN ORGY		$3.95
☐ Villefranche, Anne-Marie/FOLIES D'AMOUR		$3.95
☐ Villefranche, Anne-Marie/MYSTERE D'AMOUR		$3.95
☐ Villefranche, Anne-Marie/SECRETS D'AMOUR		$4.50
☐ Von Falkensee, Margarete/BLUE ANGEL NIGHTS		$3.95
☐ Von Falkensee, Margarete/BLUE ANGEL SECRETS		$4.50